THE
BOOK
OF THE
MAIDSERVANT

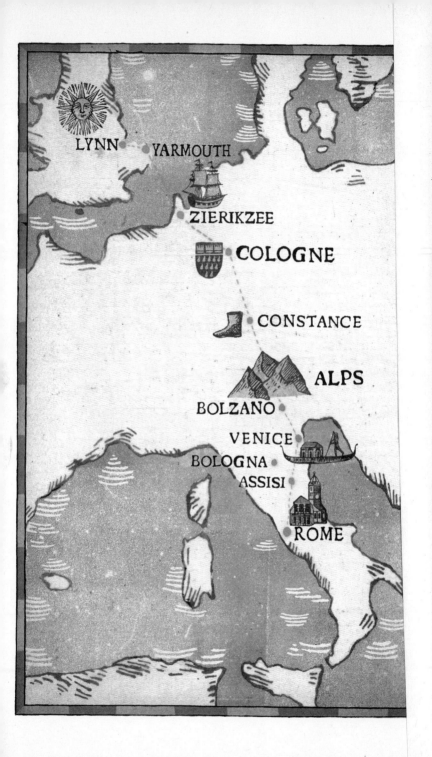

THE
BOOK
OF THE
MAIDSERVANT

REBECCA BARNHOUSE

RANDOM HOUSE  NEW YORK

Text copyright © 2009 by Rebecca Barnhouse
Map copyright © 2009 by Grady McFerrin

All rights reserved.
Published in the United States by Random House Children's Books,
a division of Random House, Inc., New York.

Random House and the colophon are registered trademarks of Random House, Inc.

Visit us on the Web! www.randomhouse.com/kids

Educators and librarians, for a variety of teaching tools, visit us at www.randomhouse.com/teachers

Library of Congress Cataloging-in-Publication Data
Barnhouse, Rebecca.
The book of the maidservant / by Rebecca Barnhouse. — 1st ed.
p. cm. Includes bibliographical references (pp. 230–1).
Summary: In 1413, a young maidservant accompanies her deeply religious mistress, Dame Margery Kempe, on a religious pilgrimage to Rome. Includes author's note on Kempe, writer of "The Book of Margery Kempe," considered by some to be the first autobiography in the English language.
ISBN 978-0-375-85856-7 (trade) — ISBN 978-0-375-95856-4 (lib. bdg.) — ISBN 978-0-375-89291-2 (e-book)
1. Kempe, Margery, b. ca. 1373—Juvenile fiction. [1. Kempe, Margery, b. ca. 1373—Fiction.
2. Religious life—Fiction. 3. Pilgrims and pilgrimages—Fiction. 4. Voyages and travels—Fiction.
5. Middle Ages—Fiction.] I. Title.
PZ7.B2668Bo 2009 [Fic]—dc22 2008028820

Printed in the United States of America

10 9 8 7 6 5 4 3 2 1

First Edition

Random House Children's Books supports the First Amendment and celebrates the right to read.

For Sid

my mistress says you mustn't stare into the fire lest the devil look out at you from the flames. "He'll see into your soul," she says.

My mistress says a great many things about the devil.

But before cockcrow, when my mistress is still abed and I'm sitting on my heels coaxing the embers into life with my breath, I stare into the fire with no fear of the devil. The devil, I think, wakes up when my mistress does.

Before then, the house is quiet and my face is warm with the fire I'm making. I stare into the coals and the new little flames licking blue and yellow around the kindling, and I don't see the devil or the mouth of hell. I see summer and yellow sun, and in the smooth flames curling around the wood, I see clear water flowing through rushes the way it did in the stream when I was a little girl.

I've just long enough for a memory of splashing in the stream with my big sister, Rose, before the rafters tremble with the sound of my mistress stirring above.

Cook limps heavily into the kitchen and casts a baleful

eye at the upstairs room. "There'll be weeping today, you mark me," she says, and busies herself with the pots.

It's a big house, this, for my mistress's father was five times Lord Mayor of Lynn and an alderman of the Holy Trinity Guildhall, too. The mistress doesn't let it be forgotten, not by the servants nor by the goodwives of the town, for all that she's a religious woman.

"She'll be wanting you," Cook says.

I lean forward to give the fire one last breath, although it doesn't need it. For one more instant, it's summer and I'm with Rose and the sun is warming my face.

Then I rock back on my heels and stand, letting the cold air settle around me. I heave the bucket of water I've brought in and start up the stairs.

I'm halfway up when the weeping begins.

"Ah, sweet Jesu," my mistress calls out, and then she is crying in earnest, great heaving sobs. "My sweet Lord," she cries.

I hover on the stairs. Up or down?

"Johanna!" My mistress shrieks my name from her room and up I scurry. I've been here long enough to know the consequences if I don't.

I open her door with my foot, swinging the heaving bucket into the room. She's sitting on her bed, her face in her hands, the tears coming fast. The water from my bucket goes into the hand basin with only a river or so spilled out, and then her foul-smelling night bucket is in my hands and I'm on the stairs again.

"Come back, you stupid girl."

I stop. Even when she's full of the passion that Our

Lady Mary suffered for her poor son, my mistress notices things. You'd think she'd be blinded by her tears.

"The fire, Johanna."

I set the buckets down and creep into the room again. I had thought to come back for the fire later, when I brush her hair and pin up her headdress—after the weeping has abated. But my mistress likes to be warm and toasty while she shares Our Lady's pain.

The bellows crouch beside the fireplace. I mend the coals with the tongs, then blow them into flames with the bellows. Already, while my mistress was sleeping, I've brought up the coal. Also, I've scoured the bottles and pots left from yesterday. And brought in the water for Cook and for me, lots of water, fetched from the Common Ditch, a long walk through the ooze and muck of the streets in the chill damp of the morning.

My mistress feels such compassion for Our Lord, she cries and cries at the thought of him on his rood. You'd think she could spare some compassion for me. Almost June and still the mornings are cold as midwinter.

She interrupts her weeping to say, "Don't dally before the fire, you wicked girl. The devil creeps into the souls of those who dally."

She should know.

I escape down the stairs to haul the iron pots of water to the fire for washing. Linens today.

When I lived by the river, off in the Fens, after my mother died giving birth to a baby who didn't live to see the sunrise, my sister Rose did the washing. Back then, I really did dally, kicking my heels in the stream, weaving sedges together to make birdcages, trying to catch silvery minnows with my bare hands, fashioning pipes of reeds. I thought I was working, but Rose was doing it all. Now that she's married to a farmer, she knows even more about work.

Dame Margery thinks she's overburdened, what with the Lord's suffering on her shoulders, but she knows nothing of burdens. Cook and I and poor little Cicilly know about burdens. Cicilly has a cough, so Cook and I have conspired to let her sleep longer. Just so she's visible by the time the mistress sweeps downstairs.

Since our household broke up at Michaelmas—Rose going off with her farmer, my father going to harvest the bishop's fields, and me going into service for Dame Margery here in town—Cook has been all the family I have. Cook and Cicilly. Piers, who does the men's labor, treats me too ill to be family. He grabs my braids and sometimes my skirts in a way I don't like at all. Besides, he smells.

But Cook can laugh. She's a sly one, Cook is, when her joints aren't making her limp and groan.

"Come, Johanna," she says. "Here's her morning meal to be taken up. Enough for her and whatever saint is visiting today."

It's when I'm up the stairs, handing her the trencher, that my mistress changes my life again, for the second time in a year.

"God has told me to go on pilgrimage to Rome," Dame Margery says. "I'll need a maidservant. Cicilly's too young; Cook is too old. You'll go with me, Johanna."

My mouth drops open. A pilgrimage to Rome? With my mistress?

"The Lord doesn't hold with idleness. Get on about your duties," she says, her mouth full of bread.

I tear down the stairs as fast as I can.

Warm weather finally comes, and I can go out without fear of frostbite. Cook says I never did need fear frostbite, but she was warm in her kitchen while I was elbowing my way through the Saturday market, my stomach leaping with fear and excitement every time I thought about Rome.

Today I scuttle past St. Margaret's, where my mistress has gone to speak to the parson about our pilgrimage. I glance over my shoulder, but she's inside, so she doesn't see me.

Over the Millfleet and past All Saints, where the holy man prays in his anchorhold. I'm off to the marshes to gather rushes, which always makes me think of Rose and of our packed dirt floor at home that she kept so clean with her broom. The door was always open in the summer, and chickens wandered in and out, into the cool shade of the cottage and back out into the summer sun. There may have been only one room, and the fire smoked something dreadful, and the roof leaked every time it rained, but it was home.

At Dame Margery's, the wooden floors all have rushes on them, because she is rich and lives in a big house in town—so big that it has four different rooms, a staircase, and even a chimney for the smoke. It's my task to gather the old, moldy, soggy rushes with their mice and bugs and bits of meat and slimy vegetables clinging to them and throw them in the street before laying down fresh rushes.

But gathering rushes I like because I get to be alone, barefoot, under the wide sky with my thoughts of Rose and of home. And besides, there's nobody to watch me when I stop to let the minnows nibble my toes. The sharp rushes slice into my wrists, and the edge of my skirt is muddy, but I don't care. Huge gray clouds sail across an ocean of sky, and the waterbirds stalk and call to their mates. A snail, his home packed tight into his shell, sways sideways as a breeze ripples through the reeds.

Why does the holy man wall himself up inside the anchorhold, praying night and day? Once, I went with my mistress to call on him. They talked in low voices, and then the holy man reached his hand out of his window to place it on my head. I felt a tingle go down my spine. Was it a demon leaving my body? After that, I tried to be good for a long time. I didn't hide beside the church to see the lepers coming to hear Mass through the lepersquint. And I prayed all during Mass instead of watching the wart on the priest's chin wiggle as he spoke.

What would it be like to wall yourself up for the rest of your life that way, to serve only God? When I listen to the wind whistling through the marshes, bringing with it the smell of salt and mud, making the reeds bend down to touch their knees, I know I could never lock myself up in a room that way. Nor could my mistress, for all her holiness.

That makes me think of our pilgrimage and I shiver. We'll take a ship at Yarmouth, my mistress says.

Every day, ships and fishing boats come up the river to Lynn, and many's the time I've stopped in my errands to watch men unload coal and cod. On Codling Lane, I've bargained with tradesmen for stockfish that have swum in seas as far away as Norway, wherever that is. But I don't want to go to Norway. I don't want to go to Rome. I don't want to climb aboard any ship at all.

Water runs through my life. I was born by the River Gay, and for thirteen years I lived there, summer and winter. Now I live in Lynn by the River Ouse, which empties into the sea. The Millfleet and the Purfleet run through town, and I crouch in the marshes, mud between my toes, to gather rushes. And I know that people belong beside the water, not upon it.

I reach for another tall rush, and the wind whispers, "Johanna." In the distance, a gull screeches my name. From town, the sound of bells floats over the marshes. My arms are sliced and raw from the rushes, but I'd rather be here in the muck than listening to my mistress weep.

"Johanna." A small voice behind me. It's Cicilly, pale and out of breath from running. She coughs and begins to cry.

Still crouching, I pull her into a hug. "What is it, my pet, my lamb?" I smooth her blond curls back from her head, just the way Rose comforted me long ago when our neighbor's pig chased me.

"It's Dame Margery," Cicilly says, and hiccoughs. "It's her father, John Burnham. And I couldn't find you."

"Shh, shh, you've found me now," I say, wiping a tear from Cicilly's dirty cheek. "What about John Burnham?"

"He's dead," Cicilly says. She begins crying in earnest.

I drop the rushes. "May the saints preserve us." I take a deep breath. "Come on, lamb. We'd best get back."

The Guild of the Holy Trinity gives my mistress's father a funeral procession to remember. Mayor of Lynn and an alderman of the guild, he was. All the guildsmen wear their livery and carry their bright banners as they process from the guildhall to St. Margaret's. My mistress wears her finest black wool, but she doesn't weep.

Even if I had reason to weep, I wouldn't have time. Nor would Cook. We keep Cicilly running, too. Ever must I haul more fresh water from the Common Ditch. I can't find Piers anywhere, but he wouldn't help me even if I asked. "That's women's work," he'd say. Coal, firewood, more water. I carry and sweep and scrub and clean. I push the bellows into Cicilly's hands; she can blow the fire into shape while I scour the iron pots and the roasting iron and scrub the wooden trenchers and bowls and saucers. That's her job, but she's too slow for a day like today. The rooms must be tidied, the cushions straightened, the linens and towels brought in, the beds made, the table laid. Then I must go for more wine. And where is Piers?

By the time Cicilly and I climb the ladder to our room under the roof, we can barely keep our feet on the rungs, we're so weary. We collapse onto the pallet, neither of us having washed.

Cicilly sleeps immediately, but my muscles protest and fleas swim in my sweat. Sharp straw from the pallet pokes my neck, my elbows. I scratch and turn and scratch some more.

I can't stop thinking about the pilgrimage. What does the funeral mean? Will my mistress change her mind now that her father is dead? Or will his death make the trip easier for her? Cook told me Dame Margery's husband has given her permission to go on pilgrimage if she pays his debts first.

When I first came to town, I thought my mistress must be a widow. Then Cook told me that my mistress and her husband had taken a vow of chastity. "At first they lived together," Cook said, "but tongues will wag. Some said as how they enjoyed each other's bodies while they called themselves chaste."

I blushed and Cook swatted me with a rag she was holding.

"Go on there, you," she said. "I've seen you looking at Piers when you thought you were private-like."

"I never!" I said. "Not Piers!"

"Who, then?" she said, laughing, and swatted me again.

"What about the mistress?" I said.

"Well, now, she and her husband live apart, don't they? And the parish priest gave them permission."

"If Master Robert gave his permission, why do people dislike her?" I asked. I had heard people laughing when my mistress went by, and in the market, tradesmen sometimes asked me about her—and about who she shared her bed with.

"Ah," Cook said. "All that piety is wearisome; you'll find out."

I have found out. Dame Margery likes to be the most pious woman in Lynn. This pilgrimage is just another bead on a long rosary full of pieties.

I sit up in bed and hit my head on the low roofbeam, where my treasures are tucked into a knothole. I reach into it and finger the smooth brown pebble I brought with me from home and stroke my soft gray swallow's feather. The scrap of red wool that I rescued from the ground beneath a tailor's stall one market morning has disappeared. Mice must have found it. But the knife my father gave me is in its place. So is the tiny doll with the acorn head that Rose made for me when I was little.

In the still night, matins rings from Greyfriars, telling me there are only a few more hours before dawn, but I still can't sleep. Moonlight steals in between the cracks in the boards above me.

Rome! It's so far away, I can't imagine it. My father went to Norwich once, and the parson has been all the way to Canterbury. But Rome!

I clench my pebble from the River Gay tight in my hand.

I never thought I would leave Rose and my father, but here I am in Lynn, where the walls of St. Margaret's soar to the heavens, it's so big, and where my mistress's house could hold all the people from my village, it has so many rooms. Never did I think I would see a place like this, so full of people and buildings and noises and smells. Even if I did come here, I thought it would be with Rose. I thought she would always be there to comfort me.

But in my thirteenth year, after my father had the second of two bad harvests, Rose stopped being so haughty with Hodge, the rich widowed farmer who lived across the fields. "But he's so old, Rose, so much older than you!" I would wail.

"Not that old," she would say.

"But he's already got three children of his own," I'd say.

"Three lovely little boys and you'll help me take care of them," she would answer. "We'll come to love them, you'll see," she would say, but she didn't laugh as much, and she stopped singing her funny goose songs as she did the washing.

Back then, I thought Rose was the only one getting a sour deal, marrying Hodge. "But he's a good man, and he'll be your brother, and perhaps he and Father can join their fields and work them together," she said then. Does she still think Hodge is a good man, with our father working the bishop's fields and me living with Dame Margery?

Cicily rolls over and begins to cry in her sleep, fat round tears glinting in the moonstripes on her cheeks. I lie back down and put my arm around her, hot as it is in our little attic. I stroke her hair and whisper-sing a song about the Virgin to her. I'm asleep before I can finish the first verse.

3

We are still going. We are to leave by Michaelmas, just as the leaves begin to turn and the apples come ripe. Now that summer is ending, we spend all our time getting ready.

For me and Cook and Cicilly, this means endless preparations, in addition to our regular work. We're sewing sheets and hoods and greasing our boots to keep the water out when it rains. Simon, the brother of our mistress's husband, over in Skinner's Row, is making us little leather packs to hang from our belts. He calls them *scrips* and says all pilgrims wear them.

He is delivering them to Cook when I return from my fourth visit to the Common Ditch in one day. I stop just outside the kitchen door when I hear my name. "Johanna may not be a beauty like our little angel Cicilly," Cook is saying, "but she's loyal as an ox and on her way to being strong as one, too."

"Seems to me she's got a thing or two to learn about work," Simon says, just as I've set down my buckets. Eight buckets of water today and he thinks I don't know how to work?

"How's that, now?" Cook asks.

"I'm not the only one who's seen her chasing butterflies around the churchyard, if you take my meaning."

I don't want to hear any more. As I creep away, Cook's voice floats through the open door. "She works hard enough in this house, you can be sure."

Smiling at Cook's words, I turn the corner. Just this morning, she had to remind me three different times to wash the pot she needed for our midday meal.

"Johanna!"

I groan. Now my mistress wants me—me, who just hauled home two buckets of water. Why can't she get Piers or Cicilly to help her?

But, no. I'm the one who has to carry her basket to Dame Hawise's house. My mistress is visiting everyone who has bad feelings toward her. This takes a lot of visiting.

As we walk to Checker Street, my mistress tells me about her conversation with the Lord. He speaks to her often, the way a friend speaks to a friend, she says, not all high and mighty like you might expect. Last night when they conversed, God told her not to worry about what people said of her. "'Daughter,' he said, 'the people will gnaw at you just as any rat gnaws the stockfish,'" she tells me.

I'm busy pulling my skirts out of the mud in the street, trying not to step on cabbage rinds and horse dung and rotten fish, and lugging the basket. A few steps before us, Agneta Millener, her baby in her arms, puts a careful foot out as she crosses the ditch that runs through the middle of the street.

Dame Margery stops short and stares at Agneta. Her lip begins to tremble and her nose reddens. "The blessed Virgin carried Our Lord just so," she says. And then she's weeping, great howling cries.

Agneta turns and looks at us. "It's an evil spirit makes her weep that way," she says to a man carrying two chickens by their legs.

"Could be bodily sickness," the man says. One of the chickens squawks in agreement. The man looks concerned, but he keeps on his way.

"It's an evil spirit, all right," an old woman tells Agneta. "Keep your baby away from her."

Agneta's eyes widen and she hurries on.

My mistress is crying too hard to notice this talk. She backs her haunches onto a barrel outside the wineshop.

A crowd begins to gather round us. I look at them—Petrus Tappester, who owns the Cock and Hen; two fishermen; Jerold, the harvest reeve; a group of dirty little boys; and the fat woman who told Agneta about the evil spirit.

"Her pride let that evil in," the old woman says.

"Thinks she's better'n the rest of us," Petrus Tappester bellows. He bellows everything. His voice is as big as the rest of him, especially the paunch that hangs over his belt. Too much of his own ale, Cook says. She's warned me to stay away from him, but she needn't worry. I'd sooner dance with the devil at midnight than speak with Petrus Tappester.

The old woman kicks a mangy dog away from where it sniffs about her skirts. Then she shakes her finger at my mistress. "Making her husband live alone while she enjoys her body with all manner of men out in the fields," she says.

"That's not true," I say. I'm not sure about the evil spirit, but I know my mistress is chaste.

A woman in a fancy headdress leans in. "Why isn't she home with her children and her husband like a wife should be?"

It's a question I've wondered as well, so who am I to answer her? Behind me, my mistress continues to weep, oblivious.

Something hits me on the shoulder. A rotten onion. I whirl to face the group of boys. "Stop that!" I say, and rush toward them.

They scatter like chickens, laughing and hooting, and the rest of the group drifts away. The old woman continues to look back at my mistress, muttering darkly.

I take a deep breath. I'm shaking.

Dame Margery is wiping tears from her cheeks. She looks up at me. "God is always with me. He sends his angels to guard me, night and day, wherever I go."

Fine. He didn't send any angels for me, and I'm the one who got hit with the onion. I wipe at the slime on my shoulder.

Dame Margery heaves a great sigh and pushes herself away from the barrel. "That baby put me in mind of Our Lord when he was just a newborn. How his poor mother suffered when he died."

I don't say anything, but I'm thinking of what the woman with the fancy wimple said. My mistress has a lot of children, all living with their father and cared for by maid-servants and the two older girls. If babies make her think so much of God, why doesn't she take care of her own children? Then she could be thinking of God all the time.

When we get to Dame Hawise's house, I go into the kitchen with my basket of bread and stockfish. Anne, the saucy girl who works there, wipes her hands on her apron and peeks into the other room. "They'll be a while. Come on, the pots can wait," she says.

We make ourselves comfortable on the bench just outside the kitchen door.

"A pilgrimage!" she says. "Are you afraid?"

Of course I'm afraid, but not right now while the breeze flits around us, bringing the smell of the salt sea. I shrug.

"I'd be afraid," she says. "Did you hear that Petrus Tappester has to go on a pilgrimage, too?"

I whirl toward her. "*He's* going to Rome?"

Anne shakes her head. "No, not Rome. The Holy Land. The parson's making him go. And the Cock and Hen has to stay closed until he gets back."

"Why?"

"My mistress told me about it." She grabs one of her braids and strokes the tip, the way she does when she's about to tell a story. "A long time ago, when his wife died—not long after they were married—he changed. That's what my mistress says. When he was young, all the girls had their eyes on him. Even my mistress."

"They had their eyes on Petrus Tappester? He's bald!"
I say.

"He is now. But when he was young, he had lovely blond hair and fine legs—and he wore a very short tunic." She grins. "That's what my mistress says."

I shake my head in disbelief. People may change, but not *that* much.

"Wait," she says, and leans toward the open door to listen for our mistresses, but they're still talking. She settles back onto the bench again. "When his wife died, he got angry. And then he got all hollow inside." She rubs her belly and leans toward me to whisper, "So hollow, there was room for a devil to creep in."

A chicken startles me, pecking at my bare toes. I nudge it away. "Then what happened?"

Anne's eyes gleam. "It's still there."

"It is?" The chicken pecks again and I kick at it.

"The parson tried to get it out, but now he says the only way is for Petrus Tappester to go to the Holy Land."

I look at her, my eyes wide, a shiver on my scalp. "Can it get out? Before he gets to the Holy Land?"

She shakes her head firmly. "That's why Master Robert is making him go. It won't come out until he gets there."

She raises her hand to silence me and listens again. Our mistresses' voices are getting louder—they're coming this way. We scramble back inside and start wiping pots with our aprons to look busy.

On the way home, while my mistress stops at St. Margaret's to talk to Master Robert, I try to picture the devil inside Petrus Tappester. Does it have wings and a tail like the demon peeking around a corner in one of the church wall paintings?

I tell Cook all about it when we get back. And I tell her about Dame Margery. "She left me alone with all the crowd throwing things at me," I say. "All she did was cry and moan while I had to face all those people."

"You'd think they'd throw things at her, not you. Or have the saints started speaking to you, too?" Cook says.

We are brushing the moths out of clothes. Dame Margery has just given Cook an old dress, so she's pleased. She keeps picking it up and pressing it against herself, looking for ways to make it fit her better. She acts like a girl readying herself for her first Michaelmas Fair.

"And now Master Robert has given her permission to wear white, as if she were a virgin who never had a single child," I say. "I wish he'd thought about who'd have to sew all those white clothes."

Cook laughs. "You think she'd let you sew them? With your seams going every which way?"

"No. But while you're sewing them, who'll have to work twice as hard at the cooking and cleaning and washing?"

"And Master Robert didn't think of that, now?" Cook is laughing at me.

"Cicilly!" I call. "Come help me bring in firewood." Cook can brush out these clothes herself.

Cicilly comes running. If nobody else loves me, at least

Cicilly does. I glare at Cook as we go out, and she makes a show of curtsying.

"Master Robert will come to his senses any minute now, you mark me," she says, and bursts into a belly laugh. She gets to stay in Lynn instead of going on this pilgrimage. What does she care for my troubles?

the closer the pilgrimage, the busier we become. Three days to go, then two days, then suddenly, it's my last night in Lynn. I've packed my flint and bit of metal for starting fires, our cooking pot (Cook laughs at the idea of me cooking anything), and our pigs' bladders for carrying drinking water. I have my needles and thread and extra pins for my mistress's headdress. At my belt rides my knife, the one with the lark etched into the blade that my father gave me before he left home. And I bring my round brown pebble, worn smooth from tumbling in the River Gay, down from its hidey-hole in the roofbeam. Rose found it in the stream when I was a little girl. She made me recite my Ave Maria and my Paternoster before she gave it to me, and I've kept it ever since, a little piece of home. I hold it tight and pray to Our Lady before I drop it into the little leather bag at my belt.

I give my doll, the one with the black eyes painted onto an acorn face and the scrap of linen for a body, to Cicilly to keep for me until I get back.

Cook has promised she'll send Rose word about the pilgrimage, if she has a chance.

We stay up late before the kitchen fire. After Cicilly falls asleep with her head in Cook's lap, the acorn doll clenched in her fist, Cook and I sit in silence, listening to the snap of the flames. She leaves tomorrow as well, to serve in our mistress's brother's kitchen. Cicilly will go back to help her mother at Agnes Gough's house. I fear for her—she and her mother will have to make one meal serve them both, and neither of them is strong.

Finally, we wake Cicilly enough to get her to bed. Before I climb the ladder to the attic room, Cook hugs me long and hard.

With Cicilly nestled beside me, I sleep.

We travel to Yarmouth by way of Walsingham. A merchant on his way to Fakenham accompanies us the first day. We pass out of Lynn under the massive East Gate, the same path I trod a full year ago when I came to work for Dame Margery. Back then, I thought I'd be back with my family by now. Never could I have imagined going on a pilgrimage. It's hard to imagine it now, even though we're really leaving.

I look back at the fog-shrouded gate looming like a fortress behind us. Droplets of mist on my cheeks feel like cold tears in the chill air. The bells summoning the friars to their prayers fade as we get farther from Dame Margery's house, farther from Cook, farther from Cicilly, farther from everything that I've come to know in the last year.

In the distance, we see Castle Rising. We pass the path into the marshes where Rose and my father and I lived, and we pull our skirts to our knees to wade across the River Gay. Will my father ever hear where I am? Will word ever come to him, wherever he is, working the bishop's fields? Cook will get a message to Rose about me; I know she will.

For the first time in a long time, I allow myself to think about Rose marrying Hodge. She says I mustn't think ill of him, which means I can't think of him at all. Hodge is to blame for everything, for my family being torn apart, for me being sent to Lynn. Why did he have to take Rose from us? He could have bought my father's fields if he'd really wanted to; I'm sure he could. After all, he's rich enough to have a cottage with a window and a separate room for sleeping.

A thorn of anger pierces my heart, and suddenly, another memory comes creeping into my head, this one about Rose. One I don't want to remember. I shut it away as fast as it comes and think about Hodge instead. I promised Rose I would try to love him as a brother. But she didn't know what would happen to me. Nobody could have known about this pilgrimage. Especially me.

Wind rushes across the flat marshland. A heron lifts himself out of the reeds and into flight. If only I could sweep across the sky like the heron, I'd fly back home to Rose and my father and how things used to be. Instead, I plod along beside the merchant's donkey, my feet weary before we've even reached the church at Grymston.

We stop in the churchyard to eat our bread and cheese

and dried fish. I try to make friends with the donkey, but he bares his yellow teeth at me and narrows his eyes.

"He's sour through and through," the merchant tells me. "Give him honey and he'll trade it for nettles."

My mistress has lowered herself, slowly like a cow, to her knees. She must be having a conversation with Our Lord. I hope the donkey doesn't make her think of Our Lady riding to Bethlehem and start the tearfall.

The merchant goes right on talking about the donkey, not realizing the danger we're in. "A cussed beast, this one, but he'll carry the world on his back. He won't like it, mind, but he'll do it."

I wander around to the other side of the church and sit, my back against the cold stone wall. An abandoned swallow's nest hangs from the eaves, a torn and tumbling clump of twigs. In the center where the eggs would have been in the spring, a hole gapes, black and jagged.

As I bite into my cheese, a raindrop plops hard and cold onto my scalp. My mistress wears a broad-brimmed leather pilgrim's hat that her brother-in-law Simon, the skinner, made for her. It keeps the rain off her head. I am not a pilgrim, just a pilgrim's maidservant, so I get no hat.

But I do have a metal cross to carry with me. Just as we were about to step over the threshold to begin our journey, Cook pressed it into my palm and said, "God bless you, child." I've been clutching it tightly ever since, and now there's a green smudge on my palm.

I tuck the cross into my scrip next to the pebble from the River Gay and take out a hunk of hard brown bread to gnaw.

It has as much of Cook in it as the cross does. She kneaded it and baked it and cut it into pieces for our journey.

Too soon, my mistress calls for me, and we set off again. We walk all day, through marshes, across streams, past fields of flax and fields of barley, past grazing sheep and grazing cattle. At evensong, we finally come to the shrine outside of Walsingham. The merchant leaves us, and my mistress and I walk into the dark chapel. Ahead of us, lights flicker in brilliant colors, making me blink. As we get closer, we see hundreds of candle flames illuminating the jewels that surround the image of the Virgin. The air is so thick with incense that it makes me cough.

We kneel and pray to Our Lady of Walsingham. "Bring my family back together," I ask her. "Bring me safe home." When I look up into her kind eyes, I think my prayer is being heard.

My mistress's prayers certainly are. People kneeling all around us look up when she cries out, "Blessed Lady, mother of Our Lord," and begins to sob.

I try to shut out her voice, but she is too loud.

Then a priest approaches and gently raises her, still weeping. He leads her through a door, across a yard, and into a small room. I scurry to keep up.

To another priest, he says, "This is the holy woman from Bishop's Lynn. The Lord visited her in our chapel with holy tears of contrition and devotion."

The second priest calls a servant to find food and beds—not just for my mistress, but for me, too. Suddenly, Dame Margery's tears seem like no bad thing.

*   *   *

We leave the next morning without kissing the phial of Virgin's milk or even the piece of St. Peter's fingerbone in the chapel. What do we care for a mere fingerbone when we're going to Rome, St. Peter's own city?

Besides, a monk going to the priory at Bromholm says he'll guide us there, where we can pray to the piece of the True Cross. I can hardly wait to tell Cook about it. Even Cicilly has heard of the Holy Cross of Bromholm.

I skip along the rutted cart path, listening to blackbirds trilling as they rise from the marshes. When I try to whistle back to them, my mistress gives me a sharp look, reminding me of the monk's presence.

I stop skipping and start listening, my eyes on the rip at the bottom of his black robe. I don't think he knows about it. Every now and then, his hairy leg peeks out like a bearded face from behind a curtain in a mystery play, and it's all I can do not to laugh.

He's telling my mistress all about what St. Paul says of tears—that the Holy Ghost says to pray with mourning and weeping so plentiful that the tears can't be numbered.

Dame Margery weeps enough already. She hardly needs encouragement.

But the monk speaks on about St. Jerome, who says that tears torment the devil. He tells her to persevere against her enemies and to have patience in her soul when people fault her for weeping. "The Lord will test you severely," he says, "just as he tests his saints."

The monk ought to try serving Dame Margery for a day if he thinks *she's* the one who's being tested.

Just as I'm thinking this, the monk looks back at me, his gentle blue eyes catching mine and holding them. My face burns with shame, and I look down. Can the monk hear my thoughts? I trail behind, watching my dirty bare feet emerging one after the other from my brown woolen skirt. I wish I hadn't laughed at his ripped robe.

If the monk says my mistress is favored by God, I've been wrong to be angry with her when she cries. But her weeping is so loud, you can barely hear yourself praying!

I sigh and make a vow to pray for as long as my mistress. "By Our Lady of Walsingham," I say, crossing myself, "I won't think any more bad things about her this whole pilgrimage."

By the time we get to Yarmouth, I've broken my vow over five times. After five, I stopped counting.

The last time was in the cathedral at Norwich, where my mistress prayed to the Holy Trinity. By her account, all three of them got into an argument about who she should love best—the Father, the Son, or the Holy Spirit. It took the Virgin Mary and all twelve apostles to set things right. Along with a lot of weeping. When she shrieked out loud in the Lady Chapel, I lost my patience and broke my vow.

At Yarmouth, we're staying at an inn where other people who are crossing the English Sea have gathered. One of them is Petrus Tappester. I watch him for signs of that devil. I may not see it, but I can hear it—he has nothing good to say and a large mouth with which to say it.

At dinner, he tells me to serve everybody at our table. I look to Dame Margery to contradict him, but she's so busy praying she doesn't notice. Even when I bang her cup down hard enough that some of the ale sloshes out, she doesn't look up. When I stomp into the kitchen for more ale, the yellow-haired boy tending to the roast laughs.

I feel like a dog that's been kicked—I want to snarl and bite anybody in my path. "What are *you* looking at?" I say.

"Nowt," he says, and gives the meat a turn. "Wouldn't waste my spit on yon gentles, that's all."

"Why not?"

"Sinning in anger on account of them? When they'll just tread you underfoot? Here, have a bit of crackling." He hands me a piece of crispy fat from the meat, and I take it, blowing on my fingers where it burns them, and pop it in my mouth. Mmm, it tastes wonderful. I lick the grease from each finger, feeling less like a sharp-toothed mongrel, and grab more ale to take to the table.

As I'm handing the cups around, the landlord brings out the salt bacon.

"Only fish for me," my mistress says. "For the sake of our dear Lord, I'm fasting and so should any of you who are taking a holy pilgrimage." She glares at Petrus Tappester. "If you honor Our Lord who suffered on the cross for you, you shouldn't eat meat."

I stand with my back to the wall, watching as the other people look at one another, not knowing how to react. Then Petrus Tappester speaks, his voice as loud and rough as a donkey's braying. "This here woman wearing the white clothes of a chaste virgin bore her husband fourteen children."

The others turn their eyes from my mistress to Petrus.

"At least, she claims they all had the same father, but times were he was gone from home and she was still with child. And she's telling *us* how to be holy?"

"Our dear Lord suffered so much for you, and all you

can do is slander one who loves him? For shame, Petrus Tappester," Dame Margery says.

The others avoid my mistress's eyes as they stab at the bacon with their knives.

When they finish their meal, I eat mine in the kitchen where my mistress can't see. But St. Margaret knows I'm gobbling down more meat that the kitchen boy saved for me, and me on a pilgrimage to Rome.

After my duties are done, I escape the inn to offer a prayer at the Church of St. Nicholas across the square. He watches over seafarers, the kitchen boy tells me.

My mistress, her cheeks wet with tears, stands before a statue of the Virgin Mary—probably telling her who ate the bacon and who didn't.

I kneel on the cold stone floor and ask St. Nicholas to forgive me for my gluttony. "And protect me on this sea journey," I pray.

While I wait for my mistress in the cool, dark nave, I look up at the rainbow windows. Above me, St. Michael holds a balance in his hand, like the scales the pewterer uses back in Lynn. A tiny naked man kneels on one side, his hands clasped in prayer. He looks frightened and alone. It's his soul St. Michael is weighing.

When my mistress comes toward me, she sees me looking at it. "I know how my soul will fare when it's weighed," she says, crossing herself. Then she narrows her eyes and gazes at me. "But I'm none too sure about yours. You'd best think on that."

As she leaves the church, I scurry behind her, meek and obedient.

Everyone else has already left for the quay by the time we get back to the inn. We grab our things and hurry after them, the cooking pot clanking and poking into my back with each step.

I've seen plenty of ships at Lynn harbor, but never have I been on one before. I didn't know they would be so crowded and smelly. No matter where you step, you hear the creaking of the wood, as if a thousand groaning men are trapped within the timbers. Despite the crowd, there are more rats than people. I step over two who race to take inventory of our baggage.

People rush to find comfortable places to ride out the journey over the English Sea. Petrus Tappester elbows between two students in long black gowns. He aims for a coil of rope to sit on, but just as his backside reaches it, a barefoot sailor snatches the rope from under him. He lands hard on the deck and howls.

"Come along, girl," Dame Margery says, pulling my arm. She descends into the foul-smelling hold, dragging me after her. I'd rather stay above-boards, smelling the salt air and watching the clouds and the sea, but I have no choice.

Dame Margery finds a place between two barrels and kneels to pray. This time I need no urging to join her. As we pray, we rock back and forth with the waves that slap loudly against the sides of the ship.

Back and forth we rock, back and forth. My stomach begins to feel odd, and the bile rises in my throat. Suddenly, I clap my hand over my mouth and run. Up the ladder I go, between pilgrims and sailors and luggage. I reach

31

the side of the ship just in time to heave up all the crackling the kitchen boy gave me—and whatever else I ever ate in my life.

How could I have been so greedy? Surely this is my punishment for not fasting.

I lean over the side, gagging, my eyes watering, but nothing else will come up. The wind cools my hot cheeks, but the smell of pitch makes my stomach feel worse.

Someone beside me puts a hand on my arm and grips it reassuringly. "Look out to the horizon," he says. "Keep your eyes where the sea meets the sky and say three Paternosters. You'll feel better."

I try to follow his advice, but my stomach won't listen—it keeps leaping into my throat.

"Eyes on the horizon," he says again.

After three Paternosters, I start to feel a little better. I take a shaky breath and look sideways at the man. A black gown flutters in the wind—it's one of the students.

"John Mouse, clerk, at your service," he says, making me a mock bow. He's no older than my sister, and his eyes are brown and merry.

"Thank you, John Mouse, clerk." I look quickly back at the horizon lest the sick feeling return. The pewter gray of the sky and the pewter gray of the sea run together in the distance. Waves black in the center and gray on the edges chop the water, each wearing a wimple of white at the crest.

Behind us, the green hills of England recede.

The reality of our pilgrimage hits me in a way it hasn't

before, taking my breath away. Will I ever see my home again?

I wish Cook were standing beside me, and Cicilly, too, with my arm around her. I wish we were all back in the kitchen, sitting beside the fire. I wish I were still a child, snug in our cottage beside the stream, with Rose and my father to protect me.

I look in the opposite direction, to where we are headed, and see nothing but the waves, endless gray and shadow.

morning finally comes. We have survived the night and the voyage. My mistress kneels to kiss the ground as soon as she crosses the gangplank, forcing a crowd of people to wait behind her until she gets up again. I eye them as they shuffle impatiently. A man calls out, "Hurry up, there!" and I tug on Dame Margery's sleeve. But she's speaking to the Lord, so she pays me no mind.

Then John Mouse steps forward. "Come, my lady, the Lord has seen us safely across," he says. He talks gently, as if my mistress were a nun—and a lady, too!—and he helps me move her out of the way. I'm about to thank him when another black-robed student speaks to John Mouse in a voice too low for me to hear. I watch as the two of them disappear into the crowd.

Zierikzee is as bustling as Yarmouth. Although I didn't sleep at all during the night, and although my knees are still weak from the fear of drowning, and although my body still feels like it rocks back and forth with the waves, I can't stop looking and listening. Some people speak words I can't make out no matter how hard I listen. I almost think

I understand, and then I realize I don't at all. They must be Zeelanders.

Everything looks so different—the clothes and the flowers and the houses. It even smells different here, in a way I can't put into words.

A group of pilgrims gathers at an inn for dinner. I don't know why Petrus Tappester is here except to bedevil me and my mistress—he's going to the Holy Land, not Rome. Besides him, there are four others: a priest, an old man with a pretty young wife who I thought at first was his daughter, and their serving man, who stands in a corner watching them. He's older than me, maybe my sister's age. I'm glad I'm not the only servant.

Just as people are finding their places on the benches, John Mouse and the other student walk through the door. I smile at him, but I don't think he sees me.

While I rush around serving, I listen to the conversation—everyone's talking about where they're going.

My mistress smoothes her veil. "The Lord told me to travel to St. Peter's City," she says. "And to go by way of the Three Kings' shrine in Cologne. And Assisi, too," she adds. "That's why I'm taking the Venice route, with those of you journeying to the Holy Land."

I stare at her. Doesn't she know about Petrus Tappester and his devil?

He gives me a look, and I duck into the kitchen, my heart pounding.

When I come back out, the priest is showing off his broad-brimmed pilgrim's hat, one just like my mistress's but older and covered with metal badges. "No, that's from

Canterbury, the shrine of the holy martyr," he says, ducking his head. He's round and shy, and his blond lashes flutter whenever he blinks. "The scallop shell, that's from St. James, in Spain." He passes the hat around the table. "And," he says so softly I can barely hear, "what about you, young scholar?"

I stop, a pot in my hands, as John Mouse speaks. "Thomas and I"—he gestures toward the other student—"we're pilgrims to the holy shrine at Bologna."

The priest blinks, then blinks again. "To Bologna?" he asks, confused. "To what shrine?"

John Mouse grins and elbows Thomas. "We think it's a shrine—the university at Bologna, famed for its teaching of law."

A burble of laughter escapes my lips; I don't know why. My mistress scowls at me and motions for me to serve the soup. As I step forward to fill her bowl, John Mouse catches my eye and winks. I busy myself with the ladle.

"You're not pilgrims, then," the old man says. "What are you doing here with us?"

"But, my dear," his young wife says, placing a calming hand over his, "to get to Bologna, they'll need to go to Venice, just as we will. And there's safety in numbers."

"Aye, that's true enough," Petrus Tappester says loudly. "You never know what we'll come across among these foreigners."

I scurry back into the kitchen to get away from his voice. I'm more afraid of him than any foreigner. I hate the way his eyes follow me. Can that devil inside Petrus see me through those eyes?

When I come back out with a loaf of bread, he's pulling out a little cloth bag that hangs around his neck. "The parish priest, he wrote down all my sins on a bit of sheepskin. I'm supposed to lay it on the altar at the big church in Jerusalem and then say fifty Paternosters. But I can only count to five!" He roars with laughter, but no one else makes a sound.

After a moment, the priest flutters his lashes and coughs lightly. "And you, good sir?" he says, looking at the old man.

"Well, yes, we're on a pilgrimage to the Holy Land. My wife—" He starts to put his arm around his young wife, but she turns to him, her face flushed.

"It's none of their affair," she whispers through clenched teeth.

The old man looks at her. "My dear, it's no secret at all." He looks around the table. "We wish for a child, an heir."

"Then you *must* go to the Holy Land," Dame Margery says, leaning forward to try to grasp the young wife's arm. She jerks her hand away, but my mistress goes right on talking. "The place where Our Lord was a child, the very place where his holy mother conceived, oh, yes, you must go and pray to the Virgin there." She drops her voice, but everyone can still hear her when she says, "And I can give you a few hints about things that might help."

Petrus barks out a laugh. "You can bet she'll do that. I'm telling you, this pretend-virgin wearing these white clothes knows how to get children."

"You're hardly one to talk, Petrus Tappester," my

mistress snaps, her face fiercer than I've ever seen it. "Your envy will be your downfall."

"Come, come, we mustn't quarrel on a holy pilgrimage," the priest says in a timid voice.

"Who's telling who what to do?" Petrus yells.

At that moment, a man clad in red and blue steps into the room. His black beard forks in the middle, and he wears a green cap. Even Petrus Tappester stops talking to look at him.

"They said you were bound for Venice," he says, and people nod. "You'd be wise to follow me. I've been this route more times than most."

"Are you a merchant, then?" John Mouse asks, and the man nods.

Petrus Tappester rolls his eyes, but the young wife says, "Well, as I've said, there is safety in numbers."

People rumble their agreement and slide down the bench to make room for the merchant.

Now that everyone has been served, I find an out-of-the-way spot in the kitchen to slurp my soup. As I eat, I think about John Mouse's friend Thomas. His eyes and face are as guarded as John Mouse's are open. Thomas's short hair is the color of a haystack in the rain, and he keeps the collar of his black gown high around his neck, his shoulders hunched. The two of them spoke softly to each other during the meal, and whenever John Mouse laughed, Thomas twisted his lips in a wry smirk. How can they be friends when they're so different?

Just as I've picked the last little bit of fish from my bowl with my fingers, the servant of the old man and his young wife comes through the kitchen door. He sees me and nods. I smile at him—I hope he's not like Piers back in Lynn, never doing anything but bothering me.

He doesn't smile back, just gestures that we're leaving.

I scramble to shoulder my pack, then hurry to follow the company. The last thing I want is to be left behind.

as we leave town, Petrus Tappester takes charge because he's the loudest. Never mind that the merchant actually knows the way. Petrus walks quickly, and I'm grateful for the old man and his young wife, who slow us down.

The wife, Dame Isabel, is wearing slippers, not boots like everybody else or bare feet like me. She takes little mincing steps, crying out every time her toes meet a sharp rock. Then her old husband rushes to her side and says, "Now, now, my sweet honey bird." It looks to me like he needs more help than she does, he's so old. His hair, what's left of it, is gray and so is his wispy beard. His legs are as skinny as the skeleton's that's carved into the stone outside the guildhall in Lynn. The skeleton leads a merry dance of people, from a prince to a leper, all of them heading to the grave.

I'm glad the old man with his skeleton legs isn't leading us.

And I wish old men wouldn't wear such short tunics. They'd look far better in long gowns, like priests and students wear.

Their servant is called either Bartilmew or "boy," depending on what sort of mood Dame Isabel is in, although he's more of a man than a boy. He's big, pale-skinned, and red-haired, and he plods silently behind his lady, carrying her enormous pack as if he's her mule.

The merchant keeps himself apart from the rest of the company, as if to show he's not a pilgrim. No one would mistake him for one with his cocked hat and bright tunic. Despite his jaunty clothes, he has a sour nature. He scowls up at the sun, then scowls again when a passing cloud gives us shade. He and Thomas could have a scowling contest.

With so many people, and with the priest walking near me, I feel safe from Petrus Tappester, even with that devil inside him. Who would ever do anything wrong with a priest watching?

The fields around us are pretty, green and autumn-gold. They make me think of my father's fields when I was a little girl, before everything fell apart.

Here the grain will soon be ready to harvest. When we left Zierikzee, the road was wide, but now it has narrowed to a rough track through the fields, a path pounded by countless pilgrims. The sun-warmed earth feels good to my bare feet, reminding my toes of home.

As we walk, the students start a song in Latin. The way they laugh at the end of each verse makes me wonder if what they sing is bawdy. When the priest, Father Nicholas, casts a disapproving eye at them, I know I'm right.

The priest's look doesn't stop the song, and it makes me happy to hear them sing. I watch John Mouse's brown curls bounce whenever he and Thomas skip-leap together at a certain note in each verse. John Mouse's eyes sparkle, and once he catches me watching him and grins. I smile back. I wish I could sing along with them, the way I used to sing with Rose and with Cicilly and Cook, but it's a scholar's song, something I don't know.

We pass a farm, and a dog races out to bare his teeth and growl at us. The old man raises his pilgrim's staff, and the dog clamps his teeth around it. The young wife squeals, the students laugh, and three sturdy-looking farmers come running from a field to claim their beast.

When they've grabbed the dog and the old man has shaken his staff at it to show he's the master, one of the farmers ducks his head at us and says, "Got greet you." His words sound old and clipped, but I can understand him. He must realize we're pilgrims.

"Benedicite, God bless you," Father Nicholas says, crossing himself, and then we set out again, the dog safely held by its real masters.

The river is worse than the dog. No bridges are in sight, nor any boats. We walk back and forth along the banks, looking for a place to ford it. Finally, Petrus Tappester plunges in. The water never goes above his thighs, so the rest of us follow.

I look around, and when nobody's watching, I tie my skirts up the way I used to when I helped my father in the fields. The water is colder than I expected, and the current pushes against me.

When I hear a scream, I look up to see the young wife, her large skirts caught in the current. It takes her husband, her servant, and a lot of squealing to get her across.

Then Dame Margery plunges in. When I see her teetering, I rush back and take her arm. She grabs at me and I pull her across, then quickly lower my skirts before anybody sees.

After the river, everyone is snappish. The students stop singing, and we hear nothing but the squelching of wet boots.

Then my mistress adds her voice to this song. She walks alongside Father Nicholas, but her words are loud enough that everyone can benefit from her sermon.

She says that on a pilgrimage, we should all try to be like Christ. "Don't we journey for the sake of Our Lord? Shouldn't we be as much like him as we can?"

Nobody says anything, but they all keep their eyes down.

"On a pilgrimage, we shouldn't laugh or joke," Dame Margery says. "Instead, we should speak only of religious subjects. I myself would rather be chopped up as small as meat for the pot than not speak of Our Lord and his sufferings."

Sometimes I'd be willing to do the chopping.

The priest blinks several times. "Laughter in and of itself is no bad thing." He clears his throat. "After all, as Scripture tells us, Sarah, the mother of Isaac, is known to have laughed."

I wish John Mouse and Thomas would start singing again. My mistress might go on all day long if someone doesn't stop her.

No one does.

By the time the sun has begun to dry our clothes, she

has told us all about Christ's sufferings on the way to Calvary. She says we should be suffering just like Christ did.

Aren't we?

Petrus Tappester grows angrier and angrier, yelling, "Quiet, woman!" every few steps. It only makes my mistress louder.

The afternoon goes on forever, and my pack gets heavier and heavier. My legs ache, my feet hurt, and I want this pilgrimage to be over.

Finally, as the sun sinks below a line of trees, the sound of dogs barking and a bell tolling in the distance tell us we're coming to a village where we can stop for the night. As we get nearer, we see gravestones outside the church, dark and bent like Petrus Tappester's teeth. We skirt a newly dug grave, the soft earth mounded high the way it was when they buried my mother. I can't remember anything about her funeral except the brown earth raining down on her white winding sheet.

The thought brings sudden sharp memories of home, before Hodge began stopping by. On warm evenings, Rose and I would haul the wooden table outside the cottage door. She would set supper on it while I ran to our neighbor's to exchange eggs for ale. Then my father would come home, his hair flecked with bits of straw, dirt settled into the sunburned creases around his eyes and the three long furrows across his forehead.

He and Rose would sit on our bench, and I'd take my porridge to crouch in the doorway. Their voices would rise and fall softly like the breeze that would tug at my eyelashes and pull stray hairs from my braids. The sound would mingle with the distant lowing of cows and the clanking of cowbells, and although I wouldn't hear my family's words, I would be held close in a net of comfort.

I miss them so much. I open my eyes wide to keep my tears inside.

Just beyond the graveyard, two crows battle over a bit of bone. Whose?

In the village, there's no inn or tavern, but the villagers make us welcome with bread and cheese and ale. The parson escorts Father Nicholas away, while a well-dressed matron takes my mistress and the young wife by the arm and marches them into her house. When I try to follow, she holds her hand out to stop me, then points to the barn.

She wants me to sleep in the barn, alone among all those men? I stand in the twilight watching as my mistress disappears through the door. She doesn't say a word to me; she never even looks at me.

I glance back at the barn, take a deep breath, and move toward it. I try to slip in quietly so the men don't see me. It's so dark I can barely make them out—but I can hear them joking in loud voices and pissing in the straw. After a few moments of blinking, I can see again. I tiptoe to the ladder that leads to the loft at the far end of the barn. Just as I start to climb it, Petrus looks up. He elbows the merchant in the ribs and makes rude noises.

I catch my breath. I wish Cook were here. She wouldn't let any harm come to me, even if she does tease me beyond all bearing. A chill encircles my waist like a cold eel twining itself around me.

Then John Mouse sees me. He makes a great show of

yawning, walks over to the ladder, and spreads his cloak on the straw beneath it. "Quiet down, lads. I'm trying to sleep," he says.

I scramble the rest of the way up the ladder.

As I roll myself in my damp cloak and settle into the straw, I pray to St. Pega and her brother, St. Guthlac, who lived in the Fens like I did and who were always wet and always tormented by devils. A prayer for Cook and for Cicilly; one for Rose and my father; one for my mother and the baby who died with her, God keep their souls from torment. And one last prayer for my safe homecoming.

I reach into my scrip for the pebble that Rose gave me. I turn and turn it in my fingers, like the way it tumbled through the waters of the River Gay until its sides were feather smooth. Slowly, I relax.

a slant of sunlight steals into the hayloft, sliding under my lashes and turning the straw to gold. I stretch and yawn, then hurry down the ladder to find my mistress. Even if she's sleeping inside a house, she'll want me to pin up her hair and her wimple.

I stop at the last rung, looking for a place to step between Thomas and John Mouse. They lie curled like caterpillars in their black robes, one on either side of the ladder. When my foot touches earth, Thomas starts, turning suddenly. Seeing it's only me, he blinks, closes his eyes, and curls back into sleep.

I'm not the only one up. Bartilmew gives me a nod as I creep out of the barn. He's carrying a pot of water to the old man. He's so covered in straw he looks like a scarecrow, and I'm sure he doesn't know it. I giggle as he passes me.

Then I look down at my skirt. If Bartilmew is a scarecrow, I must be a haystack. I brush at my gown and comb my fingers through my hair.

When we are all finally ready to go, I heave my pack

onto my shoulder and groan. It feels as if a hundred-pound weight has been added to it. I drop it heavily to the ground and rifle through it, rearranging things so the blankets will be between the cooking pot and my backside. There's nothing new in it—it just *seems* heavier.

The pot clanks against something as I walk, putting a rhythm into my head that soon has me humming Rose's chicken song.

Bartilmew falls in beside me, his feet keeping time with my song, but he doesn't join in. When I've hummed my way through the last verse, I ask him where he's from.

He mumbles something.

"What?" As I turn toward him, he blushes.

Working his mouth laboriously, he speaks again. "Dumpling Green."

Now I know why he prefers silence. His words are so garbled and misshapen I can barely understand them.

"I served my mistress's father, now her," he says. *Mistress's* is almost more than his tongue will handle. "She is a good lady."

Good? Dame Isabel? I haven't seen much evidence of it, especially the way she squealed like a pig when we crossed the river or the way she calls Bartilmew "boy" whenever she pleases, but I keep my mouth shut.

Bartilmew doesn't ask about me or my mistress, and I can't blame him. We walk along quietly, listening to our feet hitting the dirt. It's not a bad kind of companionship. My mistress could learn a thing or two about silence from Bartilmew.

Just as I think this, she raises her voice in a loud

conversation with the Lord. She must think someone as old as God is getting deaf.

"Hold your noise, woman," Petrus Tappester yells back at her from the head of the line. It does no good. The two of them squabble back and forth until we stop for a midday meal.

Our days settle into a pattern. In the mornings, tempers are mild, but by the time we stop to eat, somebody is angry— usually at my mistress. Sometimes *everybody* is angry at her. Especially me.

I know she's been specially chosen by the Lord, who speaks to her every day. But when he tells her what every- one *else* should do, and she passes it on to us, I am tempted to anger, even if it's a deadly sin.

Sometimes I'm more than tempted.

Does a day ever pass when the Lord doesn't tell her how wicked I am? Why doesn't he tell me, not her, if I'm that bad? Maybe I've been a little too slow some mornings or pulled my mistress's hair a little too tight when I braided it, but I hardly have a chance to dally when we walk all day from cockcrow to sundown.

It's gotten so cold in the mornings that I'm wearing my boots and my hood now, not carrying them. My legs have grown accustomed to walking for hours at a time, my back and shoulders to the weight of my pack. But my feet will never get used to my boots. The blisters they've caused now have blisters of their own. I tear little strips of cloth from the bottom of my shift and wrap them around my toes. Sometimes it helps. But my shift is getting shorter just when I need it for warmth.

Three days pass, or maybe four. One night, dusk overtakes us when we're nowhere near a village or even a farm, and we have to sleep under the stars. This sounds like fun until I'm trying to start a fire. It's nothing like blowing a banked kitchen fire back to life of a morning—instead, I have to make a flame from nothing. I've found enough wood and kindling, but no matter how hard I hit my metal strike-a-light against my flint, I can't get a spark. Twice I cut myself on the sharp flint and have to suck the blood off my thumb.

I look up to see Bartilmew watching me. He comes over, takes the flint and metal from my hands, and holds them up so I can see. "Fast, not hard," he says, and hits them together. A spark leaps to the char-cloth, lighting it, and before I know it, Bartilmew has a fire burning.

After we've eaten and I'm cleaning up, the priest tells a story about the time he saw a bishop exorcise a boy who was possessed by a demon. I glance at Petrus Tappester, but he doesn't say anything, just picks at his teeth with a dirty fingernail.

"What did the demon look like?" Dame Isabel's husband asks, placing a protective hand on his wife's arm. She shakes it away irritably.

"It was about this big," Father Nicholas says, measuring a span with his thumb and fingers. "With wings like a bat's and a tail as long as its body."

"What happened to it?" Thomas asks.

"It flew right out of the little boy's mouth and perched

on his shoulder. Then the bishop sprinkled holy water on it, and the demon vanished in the blink of an eye."

"What about the little boy?" Dame Isabel keeps her eyes on John Mouse, who is stretched out against a tree, his arms folded behind his head, his long legs crossed.

"When the demon disappeared, the boy started laughing," Father Nicholas says, "because the Holy Spirit filled up the place where the demon had been."

"Our Lord is ever merciful," my mistress says.

Petrus Tappester kicks at a stone and walks out of the firelight. I watch the shadows the flames cast on his face and bald pate. I can't imagine the Holy Spirit ever filling him, but it would be fun to see the demon leaving his body.

Long into the night, when I'm lying on the ground with rocks biting into my back, images of Petrus's demon haunt me. Does anybody besides me know it's inside him? I shudder and pull my blanket up over my face. I'll never sleep.

But when the sky begins to grow light and the birds begin to call from the fields, I wake up and realize that I have slept, after all.

Late the next afternoon, we come to a town as big as Lynn with a hospice for travelers. Everybody else is as tired as I am, and we crowd through the door.

I slide the pack from my shoulders with a sigh of relief and lower myself to a bench. My break doesn't last very long.

The hospice has a buttery for travelers to use, and the

merchant brings me two rabbits and a handful of carrots and onions he has bought.

"You've got a pot. Cook these up for everybody," he says, plumping them down in front of me. I look at my mistress, but she's disappearing through the door, off to find a church where she can hear evensong.

In the buttery, I stare at the bloody brown fur of the dead rabbits. Cook has always done this, and before her, Rose. I don't know how to skin a rabbit.

A man who is preparing his own meal takes pity on me and shows me what to do. "Squirrels are easier," he says. "Just step on the tail and pull the body out."

When he has to show me how to cook the rabbits, too, he begins to lose his patience. "After you put in the turnips, boil it as long as it takes to say a Miserere or two," he says.

I don't know the Miserere.

"Then a couple of Paternosters. You do know your Paternoster, don't you?" By the way he frowns, I can tell he wishes he had kept his mouth shut.

Dame Isabel and her husband bring wine to the table, and Father Nicholas contributes a thick round loaf, but John Mouse and Thomas are nowhere to be seen when I take the brewet off the fire. They're wise to stay away—I'm not sure whether anyone will be able to eat it. The carrots and onions have turned to mush, but I think the rabbit meat might still be raw. Little clumps of fur and gristle float on the top of the broth.

Just as everyone is finding a place on the buttery's

benches, my mistress returns from church all puffed up with holiness. "We shouldn't drink wine, not on a holy pilgrimage," she says. "And no meat, either. We should be fasting. Our Lord—"

"Quiet, woman," Petrus Tappester growls. "Your fool of a husband put up with your nonsense, but you aren't home in England. Now let us eat in peace."

"Our Lord God is as great a lord here as in England," Dame Margery says.

"I said *quiet*!" Petrus bangs his fist down on the wooden table. The pot of brewet teeters, then falls face-down onto the dirt floor.

"Now look what you've done!" Petrus yells.

"God's blood!" the merchant says. "You've ruined our supper and now you ruin our peace."

The brewet may be seeping into the dirt below the table, but my mistress didn't ruin it. I did when I cooked it. The company doesn't know how lucky they are.

I take a chunk of bread and slip out into the twilight and make my way to the stable. Through the wall, angry voices rise and fall like the wind in a storm. My mistress wails and cries.

I crouch in the dark, surrounded by the smell of manure and dusty straw, and think of home. The merchant's packhorse must recognize me. It snuffs at me, and I stroke its nose a few times before it snaps at my fingers.

When the shouting stops, I creep back into the buttery. Petrus grabs me as I go through the door. "She's with us," he says, holding me by the arm. "We need someone to cook and wash." His thick fingers grip just above my elbow, and he pulls me up against him. I try to pull away, but he grips me harder.

I look across the table at my mistress. She stands alone, red-faced and weeping. On my side of the table, the merchant glares at my mistress, and the old man shelters his wife with his arm. Bartilmew is just behind them, but his face is hidden in shadows. Where is Father Nicholas?

Petrus yanks on my arm as he speaks. "We're sick of you and your preaching. From this night on, you go your own way. Agreed?" He looks at the merchant, who nods, then at the old man, who looks down.

"Yes, of course," Dame Isabel says. "She can't travel with us anymore."

What about me? "Dame Margery," I start to say.

Petrus Tappester pulls me through the doorway, then shoves me toward the stables.

As I reach the stable wall, I whirl toward him, my eyes wide.

"You stay away from her, you hear me? Or you'll get what's coming to you." He shows me his fist, then pivots toward the hospice.

I stand just outside the stable as darkness falls around me, my breath coming in ragged gasps. They can't really leave my mistress, can they? And take me with them? Tears fill my eyes. I don't know what to do.

I hate Petrus Tappester, even if it is a sin. I *hate* him.

A noise makes me start. I slide just inside the stable door and listen.

Singing—someone is singing. In Latin.

John Mouse and Thomas come around the dark corner, supporting each other as they stumble and laugh.

I take a deep breath and step out. "Beg pardon, John Mouse. I must speak to you." My voice cracks.

He squints in the darkness and peers at me. "Ah, the little serving maid," he says. He is drunk.

"Please, I need help," I say, tears filling my eyes again. Is there anyone I can trust?

"Stay, Thomas," John Mouse says. "A maiden in distress. 'Tis our lot to rescue her from the dragons that assail her chastity." They both laugh, and Thomas pulls an imaginary sword from its scabbard.

"It's my mistress, Dame Margery," I say.

"The quiet one? Never says a word about God?" John asks.

"They've thrown her out of the company. They say she can't travel with them anymore. And they say I have to cook and wash for them."

John Mouse stands a little straighter and stops laughing. "Hush, Thomas," he says. "When did this happen?"

"Just now," I say.

"Not to worry, little serving maid," he says. "Come, Thomas, my good fellow. Bring that wineskin. Time for a disputation."

The two of them disappear into the hospice, singing again.

Fearfully, I creep into the stable and curl up in a corner to wait out the night.

9

the nickering of a horse awakens me. Light filters through chinks in the stable walls—it must be morning.

I look around, trying to understand where I am.

Suddenly, I remember last night. Where is my mistress? I gather my skirts and fly out the door, then stop when I hear voices coming from the hospice.

When I peer in, I see Dame Margery standing against the wall, her head down. She has pinned her headdress herself—and very badly. Her crooked wimple makes her look like a madwoman.

Everyone else sits on benches watching her. Everyone except John Mouse, who paces back and forth, his long black gown billowing when he turns. He gesticulates toward my mistress as he speaks. I see no signs of last night's drunkenness.

"As Christians, as pilgrims, how can you leave a woman alone in the middle of a strange country?" he asks. "She doesn't speak the language; she doesn't know her way. She may have been sent by God as a penance for us all." He looks directly at Petrus Tappester, who snorts and looks away.

I listen in awe. John Mouse doesn't need to go to the university at Bologna. He's a good lawyer already.

"Well, I'm not a pilgrim," the merchant says. "I don't have to put up with her caterwauling."

"I answer to my parish priest, not this devil in women's clothing," Petrus Tappester says. "Besides, Holy Church says women can't preach. She could get us all thrown in jail."

I hold my breath, watching. Will they still kick her out of the company with John Mouse here? What will become of me?

"Nor are Thomas and I pilgrims," John says, looking at the merchant. "But even so, we know our duty to our fellow Christians." He turns to Petrus. "Canon law forbids a woman to preach, as you say, but to pray? Heed the words of the apostle, who tells us we should pray without ceasing." He turns back to the rest of the company. "We should all pray as much as Dame Margery does, whether we're on a pilgrimage or not."

Nobody says anything for a moment. My mistress keeps her head down, but tears glint on her cheeks. I hope she doesn't start crying out loud. If she does, we're both lost.

Suddenly, Dame Isabel rises. "John Mouse is right, as befits a scholar," she says, casting a simpering smile at him.

Now the priest stands. "We cannot abandon one of our flock here in a foreign land," he says. He blinks and looks around. When he sees Petrus scowling at him, he sits down in such a hurry that he misses the bench and lands with a *whump* on the floor.

He looks up, his mouth wide with confusion.

Petrus laughs out loud. Then the merchant begins to laugh, and then John Mouse. Finally, everyone is laughing except for my mistress.

Father Nicholas smiles sheepishly, and Thomas extends a hand to pull him to his feet.

"All right, she can stay for now," Petrus says. "But no more of this wailing like a banshee, and no telling me about *my* sins. And no preaching, either."

"Especially not during meals," the merchant adds.

"Agreed?" Petrus says, looking around at each member of the company.

When no one says anything, Petrus adds, "Agreed, then." He points at Dame Margery threateningly and walks out of the hospice.

I scurry over to my mistress. She's meek like a child who has been scolded. I comb her hair and braid it, then pin her veil and wimple again. She sits quietly with her eyes lowered, her hands in her lap. When she doesn't say anything, I bring her some of the hospice's porridge and sit beside her while she eats it.

That was too close. What would I have done if they had taken me away from her?

Dame Margery is quiet all day. I walk beside her, worrying about her—and about me. Once I see tears trickling down her cheeks, but she makes no sound.

Maybe she really can change. Maybe she can be a quiet

holy woman instead of a loud one. Especially if she has Petrus Tappester threatening her all day long.

Then the merchant's packhorse lets out a long whinny, and I think my mistress can no more contain her noise than the horse can his. He twists his ears at a fly and looks about evilly. I can hardly blame him, with all the baggage the merchant has strapped to his back. Just then, my cooking pot pokes me. Who has it worse—me or the horse?

In the afternoon, we come to a river, wide and swift and brown, tangles of low, red-gold trees and bushes lining its bank, and sticks and branches rushing past in its current. It looks deep and dangerous.

"We'll have to ford it," Petrus says. "Follow me."

"No," the merchant says.

"No? What do you mean, no?" Petrus says, his fingers clenching into fists. "Who are you to tell me what to do?"

The merchant ignores him, looking one way down the river, and then the other. Finally, he nods and points. "This way. There's a bridge."

To follow him, we all have to walk past Petrus Tappester. "Where's this bridge? I don't see anything," he says.

I don't see one, either.

We go at least a mile, Petrus taunting the merchant as we walk.

Then the river bends, and Father Nicholas calls out, "Look! Up ahead, see?"

Through the trees, I catch sight of a stone bridge arching over the water. Our pace quickens as we rush toward it. I think everyone except Petrus is as relieved as I am that we don't have to try fording the river.

As we near the foot of the bridge, we can see three men standing beside the steps. When Petrus Tappester reaches the steps, one of them lowers his pike to bar the way.

Soldiers. But soldiers who serve no king or army. Two of them wear battered metal helmets, and one has pieces of metal plating tied to his chest to serve as armor. All of them have several weeks' worth of beard and grime on their faces. A crossbow leans against the leg of the man with the pike. The other two grasp daggers in one hand, swords in the other.

My mistress stops short at the sight and pulls me around in front of her. We both stand stiff with fear. I've heard stories about men like this.

The man with the pike has one eye pulled into a sightless squint. He growls something, and we all look at each other. I edge closer to my mistress. Even if I can't understand the words, I fear the tone.

"Mercenaries," Father Nicholas whispers.

Dame Isabel clutches her husband's arm.

Then the merchant steps forward, one fork of his black beard held firmly in his hand. He says something in another language, and the men blocking the bridge laugh. The merchant laughs along with them. He turns to us. "A small bit of coin might grease our way."

"Who are they to charge us?" Petrus says loudly. "They don't own this bridge."

"Ah, but they're armed," John Mouse says lightly. I can't tell whether he's frightened or not. My mistress is— she digs her fingers into my shoulders, holding me in front of her like a shield.

"We can take them," Petrus says. "I've got Squinch-Eye. Who's for the one on the left?" He reaches for the dagger at his belt, and the men on the bridge tense, readying for a fight.

My heart pounds against my chest. We're no match for men like this.

Dame Isabel's husband steps up to the merchant. "Will this be enough?" As he pours coins into the merchant's hands, the men on the bridge lower their weapons slightly.

The merchant speaks to them. They laugh as they count the coins. One of them claps the merchant on the back.

The one-eyed man makes a display of moving his pike out of our way, but all three men stand watching us as we pass. The way is so narrow that we have to go single file, and still we brush against each one of them. I keep my eyes straight ahead as I walk, wrinkling my nose against the smell of sweat and garlic and unwashed clothes.

I'm just passing the last mercenary when he says something in a low rumble. Like a frightened rabbit, I rush forward, stumbling over an uneven stone.

"Careful," John Mouse says behind me. He reaches out and steadies me just before my foot lands in a hole in the bridge. I pull it back, fast. Now that I look, I see that the whole bridge is riddled with holes.

More carefully this time, I feel my way from stone to

stone, checking each one before I put my weight on it. Below me, the river rushes by, swift and unforgiving. A drunken man would surely fall and be swept away by the current.

Ahead of us, the packhorse balks, and the merchant beats it on the hindquarters. Thomas goes forward to push it while the merchant pulls.

Finally, after what seems like days, we reach the other side.

"We could have taken them, easy," Petrus says.

"We should keep going, and fast," John Mouse says, casting his eyes back at the bridge. "They know we have more money."

The merchant doesn't answer; he just sets off at a fast clip. The rest of us need no urging to keep up.

My heart won't stop hammering under my ribs. At every puff of wind, every birdcall, I glance back, long after the bridge is out of sight. Even Cook, whose thick arms can lift a heavy cauldron off the fire, couldn't protect me against those men.

We come to a village with an inn while there's still plenty of light left. No one counters him when the merchant says we'll stop for the night. "We'll need to set a watch," he says. "You first." He points at Petrus Tappester, who opens his mouth to argue and then shuts it again.

My mistress and Dame Isabel and I all share a bed with hundreds of fleas, but I hardly notice their biting. Every time I close my eyes, I see the soldiers' faces and I shudder. Every footstep makes me think it's them. They would murder us in our sleep for our money. Even me, and I have none.

Never before did I realize I might die on this journey. Silently, I pray to all my saints—Pega and Guthlac, Margaret, and Michael with his scales. I don't want him measuring my soul just yet.

10

We wake to a leaden sky and cold rain. Autumn is passing. Most of the fields here have already been harvested.

The merchant says that just because the mercenaries didn't attack us last night doesn't mean we're safe. "They could be waiting for us—be wary."

We glance at each other, our faces grim. I cross myself before I pull my hood over my head and hoist my pack onto my back. So does Father Nicholas. He looks heavenward and prays in Latin. We all wait silently for him to finish before we start out.

Our path winds through open fields, giving the soldiers no place to hide, but every now and then, we pass thickets of trees and bushes. We all grip our knives. My mistress has no monopoly on prayer today.

We haven't gone far when she puts both hands to her heart and cries out, "Oh!"

"What is it, Dame Margery?" I ask, rushing to her side.

"Those soldiers," she says.

"Yes?" I'm not the only one looking around to see what she sees.

"Just like the soldiers who mistreated Our Lord Jesu on his way to Calvary," she says. "The Lord sent them to remind us of his sufferings, to show us how we should be more like Christ."

I grip her arm. Her eyes are closed. She doesn't see that everyone has stopped, that Petrus Tappester has turned from his place at the front of the line and is stalking toward us.

"The Lord told me—"

Petrus whips out his dagger and puts it to my mistress's neck, just under her chin. Her eyes and mouth fly open.

Everyone watches, frozen.

"What did I say?" Petrus says.

No one speaks.

"We had an agreement. No more preaching. I'd advise you"—he pushes the dagger forward, making my mistress take a step back—"to remember that. *Now.*" He pushes again. A spot of red blooms through my mistress's white wimple, just where it's tied beneath her chin.

Petrus shoves the dagger back into his belt and looks around at all of us. Then he strides forward into the rain, splashing through the mud.

Silently, we begin walking again. I glance at my mistress. Her lower lip quivers, and her eyes are brimming, but she doesn't say anything.

I don't know which to watch for—the mercenaries or my mistress. I look through the rain behind us, back at her, then out into the fields. Every way I turn seems full of danger.

"Sweet Jesu," my mistress says beside me.

Oh, no. Her tears mingle with raindrops—it looks like she's working herself up into a regular crying fit.

"Dame Margery?" I say softly, soothingly.

"The Lord says I *must* speak. To honor Our Lord and his dear mother, I *have to*." She takes a ragged breath, the kind that comes right before a sob.

"Dame Margery!" I grip her arm, keeping one eye on Petrus Tappester, thinking of the devil inside him. "Mistress, the mercenaries will hear you. We have to be quiet," I say, my voice high with fear and frustration. I'm almost as loud as she is.

Ahead of us, John Mouse approaches the priest, and I hear him say, "You have her confidence, Father Nicholas. Could you try to calm her?"

Father Nicholas glances back at us just as my mistress takes another deep sobbing breath.

"I'll try, my son," he says. He waits for us to get to him and takes a place on the other side of her. He begins murmuring into her ear, so low I can't make out the words.

Every now and then, she bursts out with "Our Lady in Heaven says" or "The Lord told me," but somehow the priest is able to quiet her.

I drop behind them, watching Petrus, watching the fields for any signs of soldiers, keeping my ears taut. My hood muffles sounds, but the sodden fields around us seem to harbor no places for mercenaries to hide.

By midday, the rain begins to lessen, but the fields give way to a dark line of trees. There must be a stream ahead.

As the path winds under the dripping branches, our spines straighten, our footsteps quiet, our hands tighten on our daggers.

My mistress is the only one who doesn't notice the danger. "My Lord, I hear you!" she cries out suddenly.

If the mercenaries are hiding in these trees, they know all about us now.

Petrus is swift and silent as he makes his way back to Dame Margery, his pale eyes narrowed in anger, the veins in his nose glowing red. He leans down and in a move so fast no one can stop him, tears a swath of fabric from the bottom of Dame Margery's skirt, exposing her shift. The fabric rips with the sound of a scream.

We all watch, unmoving, as he tears the cloth again, balls up part of it, and shoves it in her mouth, then ties the rest of the cloth around her head, covering her lips to keep her from speaking. She just stands there, allowing it.

"Try to take it off and I'll tie your hands behind your back," he says to her. He glares at each of us in turn, daring us to speak. Then he moves back to the front of the line, his dagger out. He looks at the merchant, who nods back with some kind of understanding.

They set out again, advancing warily through the trees.

I don't know what to do.

Nobody looks at me. Nobody looks at anybody else— they all keep their eyes on the bushes lining the path as they follow Petrus and the merchant.

Dame Margery stands stock-still, not crying for once.

I'm last in line and I don't like it. I go forward and gently take her arm. "Come, mistress," I whisper.

She walks obediently beside me.

I watch either side of the path and glance behind me every few steps. Looking for the soldiers keeps me from seeing my mistress's face. Her nose is uncovered so she can still breathe, but she can't talk. She doesn't even try. She keeps her arms at her sides, never touching the gag.

The path winds downward, and before long, I can hear the sound of a stream. And suddenly, voices.

We stop. The merchant looks back at the rest of us, signaling us to silence, but there's no need. Even Dame Isabel holds her knife at the ready.

Slowly, silently, we creep forward.

I grip Dame Margery's arm, pulling her along, glancing behind me and wishing we weren't last.

I shudder when I remember the one-eyed soldier with the pike.

The water gets louder, but the voices are gone. Have they heard us? Our pace slows. The merchant and Petrus go first through the undergrowth, then the two students. Behind them, Father Nicholas leads the merchant's horse. Just ahead of Dame Margery and me, Bartilmew looms over his master and mistress, a stout stick in his hands.

I whirl at a sound behind me. A squirrel scampers along a tree branch. I breathe out in relief.

As we near the stream, the path turns sharply.

Petrus and the merchant disappear from view, then John Mouse and Thomas.

The priest stops, holding the horse's lead, and the rest of us stop behind him, our bodies tense, ready to run.

Suddenly, there's shouting. The water is so loud that I can't tell what they're saying, and the trees block my view. What's happening? Are there more than three soldiers?

We might die any minute. I look at Dame Margery. Her eyes are as full of fear as mine must be. Shame mingles with my fear—I can't leave her like this.

I raise my dagger and begin to cut.

The gag falls to the ground.

11

john Mouse appears from around the bend.

"Hurry!" He beckons us to follow.

Father Nicholas pulls on the horse's lead and turns the corner. Dame Isabel goes next, then her husband, then Bartilmew.

Finally, it's our turn. I pull my mistress along the path as she mouths a prayer, her lips and tongue moving silently.

When we round the trees, we can see the stream—and four peasant boys with fishing nets. No soldiers at all.

The boys watch us as we pass. One might be my age, but the other three are no older than Cicilly. As I go by, one of them sticks out his tongue at me. I grin with relief. My thumping heart begins to calm, and my knees feel weak.

At the brook, fast water chuckles around mossy rocks, and we have to step carefully to cross it. The horse whinnies and digs in his hooves until the merchant takes his lead from Father Nicholas.

Once we've crossed the water, the path broadens out enough that I can hear John Mouse laughing as he describes the way Petrus surprised the peasants, making them yell.

"Poaching, they were," the merchant adds. "Thought we were going to turn them in."

When we emerge from the dripping trees, the rain has stopped, although low gray clouds still scud across the sky. I push my hood back, close my eyes, and let the cold wind wash away the last of my fear.

Petrus Tappester's voice startles my eyes open again. "Who did this?" He points at my mistress's face.

Nobody says anything. I stare straight ahead, unable to breathe.

"I warned you," he says, pointing around at each of us. His finger comes to a stop on me.

I look down. I thought we were going to die. My mistress needed to pray. We all did. Surely Petrus Tappester can see that.

"It's about time for a break and something to eat, isn't it?" John Mouse says, more loudly than he needs to.

"Aye, let's stop for a while," Thomas says.

"I, too, believe we should rest before we continue," Father Nicholas says, blinking as he looks away from Petrus.

They begin to take off their packs and to pull out their bundles of food, all of them moving around as if Petrus weren't standing there in front of me, as if I weren't staring at the ground mouthing silent prayers to St. Pega.

"Ho, Petrus, how about some of that barley bread?" John Mouse calls out. "Where did you stash it?"

Petrus turns and stomps away from me.

I take a shaky breath and lower my pack from my shoulders, rooting through it for our bread and cheese. When I set some beside Dame Margery, she barely notices.

There's no place to sit that's not mud. I squat and chew the hard loaf.

"We'll make Cologne today," the merchant says to nobody in particular. "By nightfall, maybe. Guards at the gate, you know—they won't let those mercenaries in, I don't figure."

"But they'll let us in, surely," Dame Isabel says.

"Oh, aye. Give 'em the sign"—he crosses himself—"so they'll know you're pilgrims, and they'll let you in."

"Foreigners who don't even speak English, sounds like," Petrus says.

Thomas lifts his eyebrows. "Their German's not too bad, though," he says, and looks at John Mouse, who grins and shakes his head.

The merchant ignores this exchange. "There's a hospice run by Englishmen in Cologne. But I'll be staying at the merchant guild's own place."

"And we'll be in the student quarters," John Mouse says.

"We'll stay more than a night, then?" Dame Isabel's husband asks.

"Two or three days, I should think," Father Nicholas says.

"Since when do you make all the decisions?" Petrus Tappester says.

I watch a flock of birds winging their way south and try to ignore the bickering. At least Petrus—and his devil—have forgotten about me cutting off my mistress's gag.

*   *   *

72

It begins drizzling again the moment we shoulder our packs. My cloak is soaked through, and its edge is heavy with mud. I have to keep reminding myself of the English hospice ahead.

We trudge through the afternoon. As we do, the path widens and we begin to see people on it. We pass through a hamlet and make our way around a flock of geese. In the distance, we can see towers, black against the sky.

"Cologne!" Thomas calls out, then says something in Latin to John Mouse, who laughs.

The two of them break into song. I can't understand the words: Latin again. But I recognize the tone. Hearing them, my heart begins to lift. Tonight we'll have a dry place to sleep with no need to worry about mercenaries.

They end a verse and laugh, then, looking at each other as they draw in their breaths, start a new one. John Mouse's voice is clear and steady. I could listen to it all day. Thomas's voice is strong, but it doesn't stir something inside me the way John's does.

Dame Isabel is listening, too. I watch her watching John Mouse. When he glances toward her, her face grows red. He looks away, at Thomas, and the two begin singing with increased vigor.

When they finish the song, John Mouse trails a little behind Thomas. I sidle up to him. "What was it about? That song?"

He grins and looks down at me. "Ah, the little serving maid. Why do you think we sing in Latin? Our song might shock your chaste ears—or those of your mistress."

"But what was it about?" Surely a song so full of joy can't be bad.

John Mouse looks at me sideways as he thinks up a translation. "It's something like this," he says, and begins singing. "To drink and wench and play at dice / Seem to me no such mighty sins." The words don't fit the tune very well, but I don't mind as long as he is singing to me. *He* is singing to *me*! My fear of the soldiers and of Petrus Tappester is truly gone now.

"Never did a man I know / Go to hell for a game," he sings. He hums a measure and then sings again, "And to heaven will no man go / Because he aped a holy show."

These aren't the kinds of songs I'm accustomed to. "Stop!" I say. "My mistress might hear you."

He grins again. "You asked."

My cheeks grow hot.

"Cheer up, little serving maid," he says, and winks at me. "It's Cologne! Look!"

Bell towers rise above the rooftops, and a wall encircles the city. I can see the broad river, brown as a cow's back, and the bridge we'll cross. Just on the other side of it, I see what must be the guard tower.

"Thomas!" John Mouse calls, and dashes forward to rejoin his friend. They banter in Latin, swiping at each other's hats.

Two huge draft horses pass us, each ridden by a farmer, and John bows to them as if they were knights in armor. Thomas says something to him, and the two of them hoot with laughter.

John Mouse was so grave when he defended my

mistress. Now he is so full of fun. He is the only one of the company who speaks to me without giving me orders. I watch his black gown fluttering as he and Thomas leap about. When he turns so that his eye catches mine, he grins and my heart gives a little leap. His eyes are so bright and clear.

Suddenly, they grow wide and he grabs Thomas by the shoulder. "Petrus!" he hisses, and then, "Don't look back."

I catch my breath. The mercenaries.

"Gather close," the merchant says, keeping his eyes forward. "Once we're through the city gates, they won't touch us."

Dame Isabel and Bartilmew draw near me. The students and Dame Isabel's husband are just ahead. Where is my mistress?

I steal a fast glance behind me. She strolls along, her face distracted, her lips moving in prayer, unaware of our danger.

I slow my pace to let her catch up, my heart racing as fast as my feet want to go. Finally, as she ambles alongside me, I take her arm. "Quickly, mistress, the mercenaries."

She turns toward me, her brow furrowed. "No, child, we're safe from them."

"They're right behind us," I whisper fiercely, tugging her sleeve. "Hurry!"

Nothing I do will make her go faster. The rest of the company is far ahead of us now. Other people on their way to the city pass us, every footstep making me cringe, thinking it's the soldiers.

Up ahead, crowds of people jostle their way across the

bridge and through the city gates. Petrus and the merchant are almost there, the rest of the company directly behind them. Dame Margery goes slower and slower.

A horse-drawn cart rumbles by, and we have to duck out of the way, putting more space between us and the other pilgrims.

My whole body is taut, my fingers clenched around my knife hilt. Are they still back there? I dare not look.

As the cart passes him, Bartilmew turns and sees us.

He opens his mouth in a wordless shout. At the same instant, a hand reaches for one of my braids.

Without thinking, I swing my knife behind me. It hits something.

Someone yells.

I run.

Blindly, I push my way past two farmers. Feet hit the ground behind me, and hands grab at me.

The cart blocks the path. I splash through the puddles beside it, lifting my muddy skirts to keep from tripping.

Past the cart, past the horse, onto the bridge.

People turn and stare as I elbow my way through, my skirt held high.

My breath comes in ragged gasps.

Below me, the river. Ahead, the guard tower on the city gates. All around me, people, too many people in my path.

"Let me through," I say, but no one does.

A voice growls behind me, a voice I remember. The mercenary.

I push harder. Someone plucks at my cloak. I duck

beneath a man's basket and dodge around a woman carrying a sack over her shoulder.

The guard in the tower shouts something down at me. I cross myself and dash through the gates.

My foot hits a stone and I fall hard, the heels of my hands hitting the mud, my pack slamming into my back.

Hands grab at my shoulders.

I twist to get away, but the hands hold me firmly.

I can't get free.

"Stop. Go easy," a man says, his words slurred.
Bartilmew.

"All is well," he says, lifting me to my feet.

I look wildly behind me, but I don't see the mercenaries. My breath comes fast and sharp. Bartilmew holds my arms, as if he were calming a bucking horse. Then, carefully, he takes the knife from my hand. Without a word, he wipes the blood on the bottom of his boot.

Blood?

The mercenary's blood.

I shudder.

Father Nicholas and the merchant, Dame Isabel and Petrus are all staring at me. Never in my life did I think I would be glad to see Petrus Tappester.

Bartilmew hands me my knife back, then steps to his mistress's side.

Where is *my* mistress?

I look back again, but I can't see her in the crowd clamoring to get into the gate.

"Dame Margery," I say. "I have to find her."

"No," Bartilmew says.

"But I left her. The soldiers—"

He shakes his head.

I can't just leave her. I turn to push my way back through the crowd. Bartilmew catches my shoulder. As he does, Dame Margery comes into view, one of her arms linked through John Mouse's, the other through Thomas's. Their faces are grim as they pull her along, but she smiles as if the king has asked her to dance.

As they near us, she says, "I told you we were in no danger. The Lord protected us. He said he would."

I open my mouth, then clamp it shut. Maybe she's right. Maybe that's why I'm still alive.

The crowds push us forward into the city. We stop where the way widens out. I am too dazed to hear what the merchant and Petrus are saying. I watch, barely comprehending, as the students tear off down the street, their gowns rippling behind them like wings. The merchant points and says something before leading his packhorse in another direction.

The rest of us set out for the English hospice.

High walls rise around us, cutting off the light. From every direction, people push past, all of them speaking words I can't understand. The aroma of cooking meat mingles with the smell of rot and waste. I dodge around a steaming pile of horse dung.

No matter how wide I open my eyes, I can't take it all in. I can't take anything in. All I can do is remember the hand catching my braid, the feel of my knife hitting flesh. Everything seems so dark. I want to crawl into a safe corner somewhere and sleep.

I hardly notice when we enter the hospice. Following Dame Margery into the sleeping room for women, I place our pack on a cot to claim it.

"We'll want something to eat," Dame Margery says. "The kitchen is through there." She gives me a little push toward a doorway.

I go through it and step into a courtyard. The smell of wood smoke and frying onions tells me the way.

Stopping just inside the door, I watch the fire dancing on the huge hearth. A boy comes in another door, staggering under a load of logs, his torn and filthy leggings protruding from under the wood. He drops the logs beside the fireplace, brushes off his ripped tunic, and goes out again.

At a long wooden table, a small bald man scoops millet from a huge bag on the ground into a kettle. He looks up and sees me. "New pilgrims?" he asks. "How many?"

I count on my fingers and say "Six," before remembering myself. "No, seven."

"Well, don't just stand there," he says.

He never says another word as we cook the millet into a porridge with oil and onions. As I stir, the fire warms me, and I feel my fear dissipating, my breath steadying, the life coming back to my limbs.

When it's finally time for bed, I join my mistress on my knees to offer a long and heartfelt prayer. After my

Paternoster and my Ave Maria, I beg Our Lady to preserve me from the demons who bedevil us in nightmares.

She must hear me. I sleep like the blessed dead.

We stay three days in Cologne. On the first day, my mistress and I, Dame Isabel and her husband, and Bartilmew, Father Nicholas, and Petrus Tappester all go to the cathedral together.

When I first went to Lynn, to work in Dame Margery's house, I thought I was in a city, it was so big. I thought the square towers of St. Margaret's church rose as high as a building could. On market days, more people crowded the square than ants in an anthill, all dashing about, calling to each other, buying and selling, carrying baskets of vegetables and hens, loaves of bread, bolts of wool, pies and apples, cod and carrots. Never did I think there could be so many people.

Until I came to Cologne.

I'm not the only one who is impressed. Even Petrus Tappester keeps pointing and saying, "Look at that!"

When we get near the cathedral, we can see the scaffolding covering one side, a pile of stones and rubble below it. A few men sit in the scaffolding, but none of them seems to be working.

As we get nearer, I look up at the walls. They reach so high they make me dizzy. Carved figures gaze grandly down, and we try to identify our favorite saints by their symbols. In a stained-glass window in St. Margaret's back in Lynn, the saint holds a book and stands atop a winged dragon. We walk all the way around the cathedral, dodging legless beggars and friars and men who want to sell us pilgrim badges, stepping over muddy ditches and piles of stones and piles of dung, but I can't find St. Margaret. Nor do I see St. Guthlac of the Fens or his sister, St. Pega. I can't even find St. Audrey. I am in a strange and foreign place if they don't even know my saints here.

Then I see St. Michael looking solemnly down at me, his scales in one hand, and I feel safer.

A glint on the ground catches my eye, and I reach for what looks like a little piece of sky fallen to the earth. It's a blue glass bead. I wipe the mud off it and let it catch the sun.

"What do I do with it?" I ask Bartilmew, who is standing beside me.

We look around, but no one seems to have lost anything.

"Keep it," he says.

"Are you sure?"

He nods and I slip the bead into my scrip, where I can hear it clinking against Cook's metal cross and the pebble Rose gave me.

Around the corner, on the broad cathedral steps, a one-armed boy with a rag tied around his eyes calls for alms in a reedy voice. Beside him, a man in a ragged tunic points out the Paternoster beads and souvenirs he has placed on a cloth spread on the ground, his voice competing with the boy's. Two smiling jugglers keep eight red and black balls in the air between them, joking loudly to each other, until a priest comes out of the cathedral and shoos them away. I want to follow and watch their merry fun until one of them darts a sharp eye at me and holds out his cap for coins. When I shake my head at him and show my empty hands, he scowls and makes as if to rush at me.

My heart is still pounding as we walk through the huge door and into the cathedral.

I blink in the dimness. Candles flicker behind massive stone columns. I stumble over a woman who kneels in prayer, then follow the crowd forward. Like us, they've come to see the shrine of the Three Kings.

A deacon points people to a place behind the high altar, and we join the line of pilgrims shuffling around the shrine. It looks like a little golden church with tiny people carved into its sides, just the way statues surround this cathedral. Father Nicholas points out figures of the Virgin and Child and the emperor, who kneels to them. The emperor of what? I thought there were only the king and the Pope and then God.

When I stop to peer at the emperor, someone steps on my heel, so I have to move on. Once we've passed the shrine, we come to a little stall, right there in the cathedral, selling souvenirs. Everyone in our company buys a metal badge with the Three Kings' heads on it to sew on their leather pilgrims' hats. Everyone except Bartilmew and me. We have no money, but neither do we have hats.

As we prepare to leave, I look around for my mistress. She is speaking English to a priest, who nods and smiles at her. I stand beside them, waiting for her, but she has launched into a long story—one I've heard many a time—about the way the Lord speaks to her. Finally, ducking my head submissively, I break in to say, "Beg pardon, Dame Margery, we're going now."

She looks down at me as if she doesn't recognize me. "Go along. Father Geoffrey will see me back to the hospice."

She turns her back and walks away.

13

Where are the others? While I've been waiting for my mistress, they've gone on without me. There are so many people in the cathedral, all I can see are people's backs. I scan the crowds, but it's so dark in the cathedral that I can't find anyone I know. If I get lost here, I'll never find my way back to the hospice. A knot of fear seizes my stomach.

Then I see Bartilmew glance back, candle flame lighting his face. Pushing my way past priests and pilgrims, I run to catch up with the group. As I come alongside Bartilmew, he gives me a nod.

On the way back to the hospice, we pass the university district, where narrow streets of mud run past booksellers' shops and wine merchants and taverns, where sly-looking women in low-cut bodices leer at Petrus and Bartilmew. A man goes by pushing a cart with a little oven in it. Black-robed students crowd around him like ants to buy meat pies. My mouth waters at the aroma, and I wish I had coins of my own.

Outside one tavern, students form a circle, some

standing, some sitting on stools. They crowd around a table where one student lies on his back while another pours wine from a flask into his mouth. The crowd chants something. The chanting grows louder and faster, and some of the students begin pounding on the table in time with the words.

I stand watching until Bartilmew tugs at my cloak. "A drinking game," he says, disapproval in his voice as he hurries me along to catch up with the others.

The students cheer loudly, and I turn back to watch. The drinker has just stumbled up from the table when Bartilmew jerks my arm and pulls me out of the way—a stream of muddy brown liquid splashes into the street. I look up to see a woman emptying a pot from an upstairs window.

I'm shocked. In Lynn, we never emptied the night bucket from the windows. We always carried it to the street, and sometimes I even took it all the way to the ditch in the middle of the street. People in Cologne aren't very clean.

Around a corner, we come upon another group of students. One of them stands on a little platform speaking, and others listen to him, scowling in concentration or whispering to each other. I can't understand a word—it's all in Latin, just like the Mass is—so I look at the students. Filthy, unkempt boys in filthy, ill-mended gowns, they seem to me. I try to find John Mouse in the crowd, but I don't see him.

We go through narrow passageways under banners of laundry that flutter between buildings. We pass the river, and I look across it, thinking of the mercenaries. When we go down one street, two men shout at each other from the upstairs windows on opposite sides of the street.

I don't know how the others know where we are, but when we turn a corner, there's the hospice.

I plop down on a bench inside. It feels so good to sit for a change. I lean my head back and close my eyes.

When I open them, Dame Isabel is standing in front of me. She plucks all the hair off her forehead and eyebrows, the way a gentlewoman does, even though her husband is a wool merchant—no gentleman at all. With her hair pulled back so severely beneath her veil, her eyes turn up at the corners, giving her a pained, catlike look.

"These need washing," she says, dropping a bundle of clothes on the bench beside me and walking away.

Petrus sees what she has done and says, "Mine, too." He disappears and comes back with more clothes, which he drops on top of Dame Isabel's pile.

They expect me to wash their clothes? I'm already cooking for them. Isn't that enough?

I close my eyes again. The hospice disappears, along with the clothes, the cooking, my mistress's weeping. I'm back in the kitchen in Lynn, having a summer supper with Cook and Cicilly as the birds call in the twilit sky. Cook is laughing at one of her own jokes, and Cicilly and I are smiling at each other, happy to be eating Cook's good dumplings.

Whap!

The blow knocks me off the bench. I crawl to my knees and look up.

Petrus towers over me, ready to strike again.

"You wash those clothes, or . . ." He shows me his meaty hand.

My teeth clenched in anger, I grab the clothes and scuttle away before he can hit me again. I wish John Mouse were here to defend me.

A servant in the kitchen shows me the way to the river.

Dame Isabel's shift comes clean easy enough, but when I get to Petrus's breeches, I refuse to do anything more than dip them in the water and hang them over a bush to dry. They need more cleaning than that—a lot more.

Just as I've spread the last pair of hose over a bush to dry, the sun comes out from behind a cloud. I sit down on a grassy place beside the river, rub the back of my head where Petrus hit it, and watch the pattern of sunlight sparkling on the water.

The gleaming nets of light lure me back to Lynn again, and further back still, to the pond near Hodge's cottage, where the wind rippled the surface and Hodge's three little boys chased the ducks. My job was to keep both ducks and boys safe. Ducks I could care for, but little boys I knew nothing about. Before long, I would yell and they would cry, and Rose would come running from the cottage, slapping flour from her hands and pulling William, the youngest, into a hug. He would make faces at me over her shoulder. He knew, just as I did, that they were her family now, not me.

I remember staring at the water so I wouldn't have to see the hurt on Rose's face, her disappointment in me.

Why did she have to marry Hodge? If it hadn't been for Hodge, I'd never be here now, hating Petrus Tappester.

I focus on the patterned river water and try to erase Hodge and Petrus from my thoughts. Hodge and Petrus and that look on Rose's face.

For the next two days, I make myself scarce, hiding behind walls, disappearing whenever one of the company comes into view. I braid my mistress's hair in the morning and pin up her headdress, but after that, I run to the river and walk along its banks until hunger forces me back to the hospice. They can wash their own clothes. I'm not their servant.

On the morning we are to leave, the merchant shows up before sunrise, but John Mouse and Thomas aren't there.

"Dicing and wenching," Petrus says.

"Surely not on a holy pilgrimage," Father Nicholas says.

I'd like to agree with him, but when I remember the taverns near the university district, I'm not so sure. I try not to think about it.

Dame Isabel seats herself on a bench, folds her hands in her lap, and says, "Of course, we won't leave without them."

But when they still haven't appeared by the time the cathedral bells clang for half prime and the sun is as high as the bell tower, the merchant says we have to go. When Dame Isabel protests, her husband says, "Now, now, my sweet honey bird." She looks stiffly away from him, her cheeks flushed in anger.

Suddenly, I am filled with sympathy for Dame Isabel. She is young and as lively as a calf, but her husband is old and foolish. He never allows her far from his sight. Did she have a choice about marrying him?

"Boy," Dame Isabel says sharply, and slaps Bartilmew, who has done nothing wrong. My sympathy flees, fast as a jackrabbit.

Bartilmew stumps heavily along behind his mistress, staring at the ground. He and John Mouse must be about the same age, but they couldn't be more different. I picture the way John Mouse walks: head high, back straight, clear eyes looking at the sky, the trees, the birds flying past. His feet touch the ground so lightly that it's almost as if he were dancing. Sometimes he throws in a little skip while he walks.

He speaks to everyone in our company, long discussions in Latin with Father Nicholas, questions about our route with the merchant, jokes with Petrus. When he talks to Dame Isabel, it's always in the presence of her husband. But mostly, John Mouse and Thomas sing and talk and exchange merry quips.

A branch floats along the Rhine beside us, outstripping our pace. Where are they? Surely the mercenaries wouldn't have harmed them, not in Cologne.

I look back so often I get a crick in my neck, but I never see them.

When a cart rumbles toward us, I think they must have caught a ride—but it's just a farmer and his family.

When we stop to rest and eat, both Dame Isabel and I sit so we can watch the path behind us. And when my mistress begins to pray loudly and Petrus Tappester shouts at her to stop, I'm sure I'm not the only one wishing John Mouse were here to stop their squabbling with his scholarly arguments.

"You want another gag in your mouth?" Petrus asks.

My mistress's face grows red, but it's not with tears; it's with anger. "You never forgave me for choosing John Kempe over you," she says, her voice deadly quiet.

Silence falls over us as everyone listens.

"But I would never have married you, Petrus Tappester, whether John Kempe had asked me or no." Dame Margery stands, glaring at Petrus.

My mouth drops open. Could it be true? That Petrus wanted to marry my mistress? What would Cook say if I told her!

Petrus splutters, the veins in his nose glowing purple. "You're mad, woman." He looks around at everyone else. "It's not true! You know she's a madwoman!"

No one answers him. I remember what Anne, the girl in Dame Hawise's kitchen, told me back in Lynn, about Petrus Tappester being a good catch when he was young and about how much he has changed.

Petrus picks up a stick and hurls it toward a tree. It hits with a loud crack, and a crow flies up from its branches, squawking.

Father Nicholas is the first to recover. He picks up his pack and heads for the path. The rest of us follow along, and I see Dame Isabel give her husband a wide-eyed look.

As I walk, I keep trying to imagine my mistress as a girl and a handsome Petrus Tappester—a Petrus Tappester with hair!—courting her. No matter how hard I try, I can't picture it. Surely neither of them could ever have been young and pleasing to the eye.

Not like John Mouse. Where is he?

By evening, we've found a smoky inn with more rats than guests. As I serve the whole company, I keep my ears open for the students. Before I sleep, I pray for them.

But they don't come.

By morning, neither John Mouse nor Thomas has shown up. I don't think I'll ever see them again.

A misty rain wets my lashes as we start out. My head feels heavy; the sky is heavy; my pack weighs me down.

I miss Cook and Cicilly. I miss my sister.

The memory of Rose comes fast and sharp, like pricking my finger when I'm mending a shirt. Sudden and sharp it starts, but then it grows and fills me the way a big man like Petrus fills a shirt, stretching it to the edges. That's how the pain feels, growing and spreading and filling my entire body all the way to my fingertips. The pain surprises me as much as the tears. They course silently down my cheeks, mingling with the rain.

Does Rose ever think of me? Have Hodge and his three little boys replaced me in her heart? Does she even know I'm gone?

I close my eyes and see her standing in front of our cottage, churning, her cheeks pink with the effort, a tendril of her dark hair curling beside her ear. I try to hold on to the image, not letting the bad memories in. But it's too late—they're already there, the things she said about me to Hodge when she didn't think I was listening. I hear her voice drifting up to the loft where I was supposed to be sleeping. I screw my eyes tightly shut, trying to forget, but over and over again, I hear her voice.

When I stumble blindly over a rock, a hand steadies me. Bartilmew. When did he fall back from Dame Isabel's side to walk with me?

"Give me your pack," he says, and I do so without thinking.

He hoists it onto his back, alongside his much heavier pack, and I feel ashamed. I want to thank him, but my mouth is as full of weeping as my eyes.

We walk in silence for at least a mile before I can speak. "I can take it now," I say.

He tugs on the strap and shakes his head. "Soon."

"But—"

"Soon," he says again, and we keep walking.

I think he would carry it all day if his mistress doesn't realize he's not beside her.

"Boy!" she cries in her thin voice. "Come here!"

He looks at me apologetically, then hands me my pack and lumbers away.

Just as I take it, I hear voices. I turn.

Two dark-robed figures far behind us shout and wave as they run to catch up. My heart gives a kick. John Mouse and Thomas are safe.

I scrub at my tearstained face with my sleeve as they approach, laughing, out of breath, splashing through puddles.

"What happened to you?" Father Nicholas asks.

"We thought we'd never catch up," John Mouse says, panting.

They don't say where they've been, but they smile secret smiles at each other when they think no one else is looking. They don't mention the mercenaries. I think the merchant may have been right about the dicing and the wenching.

Especially when we stop for a meal and Thomas pretends to pray over his chunk of bread: "From a scanty dinner and a bad cook, from a poor supper and a bad night, and from drinking wine that has turned, Good Lord deliver us," he says.

Father Nicholas and my mistress look shocked, but everyone else laughs. Dame Isabel hides her smile behind her hand. She is as happy as a colt turned loose in a meadow.

If she could see her face, she wouldn't be so happy. The hairs she plucked from her brows and her forehead have begun to grow back in, black and patchy against her white skin. She looks moth-eaten, like a fur coat stored in a trunk over the summer. I hope nobody tells her.

When we begin walking again, my pack feels lighter than it has in days. A silly song Rose and I used to sing comes bursting into my head, and before I know it, I'm singing it quietly to the beat of my footsteps.

> *The hare went to market,*
> *scarlet for to sell,*
> *The greyhound stood before him,*
> *money for to tell.*

I try to remember what comes next when I hear someone singing ahead of me. John Mouse glances back, gesturing for me to continue, and now that I've got the words, I do. My voice blending with his makes a thrill run through my body, and I wish Thomas wouldn't join in, but he does. So does Father Nicholas. Finally, even the merchant starts singing, and we all keep time with our feet.

We've barely sung the last note when John Mouse starts us on "How Many Miles to Beverlyham?" He remembers every single verse. Then Thomas begins a song I learned from Cook: "Come O'er the Burn, Bessy," and the rest of us chime in with "thou pretty little Bessy, come over the burn, Bessy, to me."

This time Dame Isabel looks back at us, her eyes going straight to John Mouse, and joins in the singing, but she can barely keep a tune. I wish her husband would notice the way she looks at John Mouse and say something to her.

The scent of smoke from harvest fires in the misty air reminds me of autumn days at home. When a flock of birds rises from a tree beside our path, I finger the lark on my knife blade and think of my father and Rose—and I feel light and happy.

It doesn't last long.

In the afternoon, when the rain stops, so do we, plopping ourselves onto logs or on the ground, pulling out food from our packs.

"I have some hazelnuts, if anybody wants some," Dame Isabel says. "Here, girl, come crack these nuts open."

I look up and realize she's speaking to me. My name isn't *girl*. And I don't take orders from her.

"I said, come crack these nuts. There are plenty of stones lying about," she tells me, handing me the bag of hazelnuts.

Dame Margery doesn't look at me—she's praying. At least she's doing it silently this time.

I yank the bag from Dame Isabel's hand and begin searching for two stones. I'm tired, too. Doesn't she know that?

Nobody besides Dame Isabel and her husband orders Bartilmew around, but everybody feels free to tell me what to do. And Petrus feels free to show me his fists any time he wants.

I squat in front of a flat rock and start cracking hazelnuts. Dame Isabel is sitting on her husband's cloak to keep out of the mud, and he dances from foot to foot, wrapping his arms around himself to keep warm in his short tunic and leggings.

I bring a stone down hard on a hazelnut and pretend it's Dame Isabel's head. It doesn't make me feel any better.

I hit the stones together harder, then miss and hit my thumb.

Ow. Tears spring to my eyes, but no one notices.

When I've finished cracking all the nuts, Dame Isabel doesn't give me a single one. Instead, she offers them to John Mouse.

I watch as he bows his head in a courtly gesture of thanks and declines them.

Her face grows red, and she rejoins her husband. She doesn't offer nuts to anyone else.

Later that evening, we come to a town with a hostel for

pilgrims. The hostel provides ingredients, but we have to provide our own cook. Me.

A mess of cabbage and a heap of peas, that's what they give me. But there's nobody to show me how to cook them. And the hearth is cold. At least I can get a fire started, striking my flint and metal fast, not hard, the way Bartilmew showed me, to light my char-cloth, using the little scraps of linen and bark and grass I've been collecting to feed it. In no time, I have a fire dancing on the hearth, the flames warming my face.

No fire will help this supper, though. The peas are like pebbles no matter how much I stir them or how many prayers I say, while the cabbage turns to slime. I serve them anyway.

Dame Isabel's husband breaks a tooth on one of the peas.

How was I to know I was supposed to soak them overnight and serve them for breakfast?

I go to bed angry. I wish they had *all* broken their teeth. Even John Mouse.

In the middle of the night, I awaken. Something hovers over my face, something that feels like a winged demon. Petrus's devil? Or one looking for me?

I pull the blanket over my head and pray for forgiveness. Anger is a deadly sin. I lie awake waiting for the demon to go away, listening to the mice scampering across the floor.

the next morning, our path leads us into a forest. Finally, we're out of the rain, in a dry area. As we crunch through the bracken, I go out of my way to wade through deep piles of leaves, kicking at them gleefully, smelling their rich earthy smell. When I realize the merchant and his packhorse are staring at me scornfully, I stop. The merchant can look at me that way all he wants and I don't care, but his horse makes me feel foolish.

When I stop scuffling the leaves so loudly, I can hear the dry ones that still hang from the tree limbs. With each puff of wind, they rustle with the sound of water.

By midday, there's no sound at all except our feet hitting the ground. The wind has dropped, and the air has grown still. Too still. We are deep within the woods, following the merchant along dark trails. Does he really know the way? Branches snag my hood and vines claw at my hair. I duck and twist as the trees' fingers reach out, grasping at me. I try not to think of the tales I've heard about evil spirits dwelling deep within forests. When I see eyes peering at me from a hole in a tree, I scurry closer to my mistress.

We don't take the time to stop for a meal. All of us are eager to be out of this still, dense wood. The darkness grows heavier, the forest quieter, as if it's listening to us. The trees seem to bend toward us. When a twig grabs at my cheek, I jump, slapping it away.

A bolt of lightning illumines the dark trees. The sharp crack of thunder makes the horse neigh nervously. "We'll be wanting shelter," Father Nicholas says.

"Fine, how about that lovely tavern over there?" Petrus Tappester says.

Father Nicholas doesn't answer his sarcasm.

We are scarcely ten paces farther when another lightning bolt shows us a hut ahead of us.

"There, you see? The Lord will provide," Father Nicholas says.

"A charcoal burner's hut," the merchant says.

We race for it, pushing into the tiny space just as the storm lets loose with great gusts of rain-laden wind. Only the merchant's horse stands outside, absorbing the downpour. There's no room for him, and he's an evil creature, but I feel sorry for him all the same. I know he's afraid of the thunder.

There's not even room for us to turn around in the windowless dark. I'm pressed up against my mistress, my nose shoved into the scratchy damp wool of her cloak. Bartilmew presses against my pack. Dame Isabel kicks my ankle twice before she realizes I'm not a wall.

"Where's my flint?" the merchant growls. He strikes a spark at the same moment lightning flashes outside the open doorway. In the weird, quick shadows, I can barely distinguish the dark shapes of the pilgrims. We stand huddled and bent, like souls waiting for the fires of damnation.

"Here's a lantern, lads," John Mouse says. "Where's that flint?"

Once the lantern is lit, the shadows play wildly against the straw and mud walls. Water streams in from a hole in the thatch, and there are so many drips that we might as well be out in the downpour. I can't tell if the terrible smell comes from the hut or from us, with our dirt and our wet wool.

Outside, the wind shrieks and the walls seem to press in on us. Everyone jumps at the crack of a falling tree. As it crashes to the forest floor, I can feel the ground trembling through my whole body. Gusts of rain sweep in from the entryway—there's no door to keep out the cold water.

"Any food over there worth eating?" Petrus says.

"It's not ours to eat," Father Nicholas says.

"If we're here, it's ours," Petrus says. "Toss us something tasty."

"There's nothing but onions," Thomas says.

"Well, toss us an onion, then."

"It's not ours," Father Nicholas says again in a faint voice.

As if to agree with him, a stooped little man suddenly pushes his way in the door, jabbering loudly. Even the merchant can't understand him. He shoulders his dripping body between us, and we crush back farther against each other to make room. For a minute, I think he might be a wood sprite, not a charcoal burner—he's shorter than I am, and his sinewy arms are as dark as cherrywood.

"Oh, what a horrible, filthy creature," Dame Isabel says.

Once he's by the wall, the little man sits down, right by Thomas's legs. He says something, then pulls food out of a bag tied to his belt and begins to chew.

We stand there dumbly, not knowing what to do. It's his hut, but he isn't trying to make us leave. John Mouse speaks. "Perhaps we should eat as well."

He's right. Chewing oatcakes and apples makes us relax and forget the storm. By the time we are through eating, the thunder has abated. The cold air that follows the rain seeps through my damp skirt.

"Our host is asleep," Thomas announces.

"Time we got on," the merchant says.

As we leave the hut, I glance back at the dark little man. He's wrapped his arms around himself and curled up against the wall. He smiles in his sleep. When nobody is looking, I take the last withered apple from my scrip and leave it on the ground beside him.

The storm clouds have rushed past us to harry other pilgrims, and the sky between the trees grows lighter. When the trees themselves seem to thin out, we all breathe with relief. "Here's the path," the merchant calls out, and he sounds the happiest I have heard him.

We follow eagerly, and I barely mind the way the branches slash at my face. But soon the trees begin to crowd round us again. The merchant slows to a stop. We look at each other, and then we look into the dark woods. Where is the path?

"This way," Dame Isabel's husband says.

"No, you fool, over here," Petrus Tappester says.

"Listen," Thomas says.

"Come, it's this way," Petrus says, crashing through the woods.

"Listen," Thomas says again, and in a sudden silence, we all hear what he hears. Church bells. Behind us.

We stand listening, and then, wearily, we turn back the way we came, plodding through the dripping trees, dodging branches, fighting our way through thick bushes. Spiderwebs tangle in my hair, and I wipe them from my face, hoping no spiders still live in them. I am so tired that I want to sink to the ground and sleep, but we must keep on.

Every few steps, we stop to listen for the bells and then resume our battle with the forest.

It's growing dark by the time we find the forest edge, and we tumble gratefully out into a stubbly, newly harvested field that's dotted with haystacks. In the distance, we can see the walls of a town and the roofs inside it. Tired as we are, we break into a trot, the thought of warm food and beds goading us forward.

Sharp spikes of straw poke through my boots and scratch my legs as I cross the field, slowing me. Everyone else is equally slow, and Dame Isabel lags far behind, Bartilmew helping her along.

Dark has settled around us by the time we make it to the town gate. Even if there's no inn, we'll be happy to be within the walls and safe from whatever might come out of the forest in the night—outlaws or wolves or evil spirits.

The merchant calls out in some foreign tongue, and a man holding a torch looks down at us. The flame flickers in the wind, lighting his face with weird reds and devilish yellows. He shouts down to the merchant, who shouts back. Why won't they hurry? Can't they see how tired we are?

I rub at the scratches on my arms and legs. Food, fire, bed—that's all I want. I don't even care if I have to do the cooking.

The merchant's shouting sounds angry. So does the voice of the man with the torch. But he disappears from the guard tower, and I look toward the wooden door inside the vast stone gate.

It doesn't open.

"The devil take him!" the merchant says. "It's past curfew and they won't open the gates."

"But we're pilgrims," Dame Isabel says in a little whimper.

"Did you tell him I'm a priest?" Father Nicholas says.

"They've had trouble from the forest," the merchant tells us. "They won't open the gate for anybody." He gestures toward the field and spits. "He says we're welcome to a haystack."

A haystack?

"Foxes have their holes and the birds of the air have their nests, but the son of man has nowhere to lay his head," Father Nicholas says.

"Amen," John Mouse says ruefully. "Well, if you don't mind the mice, at least haystacks are warm. Come, Thomas." The two of them head across the field to one of the distant lumps I can barely see in the dark.

"Come along, girl," my mistress says. We don't look back to see what the others do. When we come to a haystack, we burrow holes for ourselves and climb in, careful to make sure we can still breathe.

My stomach grumbles, but John Mouse is right. We're warm and out of the wind. The hay scratches, and I can feel bugs crawling up my skirt and down my neck, but we're not walking for a change. I fall asleep, picturing John Mouse scrunching his way into a haystack, cocooned in his black robe.

·

all the next day, I scratch at bug bites. It takes me forever to get the straw from my mistress's gown, and my hair is full of it, too. So is everybody's. We all sneeze from the dust and everybody scratches themselves, even Dame Isabel.

She wants to find an inn where she can wash, but Petrus and the merchant refuse to give their custom to the town that locked us out. Instead, we wash in an icy stream, then walk for hours until we come to another town. Even though there is plenty of daylight left, Dame Isabel refuses to leave once we find an inn. Even Petrus doesn't argue with her for very long. Instead, he turns his attention to my mistress, who is once again warning the whole company not to eat meat—just as I serve the salt bacon. I scurry back into the kitchen. Let them argue. I'm just relieved to be eating warm food and to have a place indoors to scratch my bites.

But by the time we leave the next morning, I've been ordered around once too often and called a sullen child—by Dame Isabel, who should know, she's so sullen herself.

My face stings from a slap Petrus gave me when he said I didn't serve him fast enough. This was right after he'd lost to Thomas at dice. My mistress saw the whole thing, but she never said a word.

I pull my cloak around me against the chill wind and walk along behind the company, my boots biting into my toes, rocks biting into my boots. What if I ran away? I could live in the forest, sleeping in one of the tall oaks. Or I could find an abandoned hut like the charcoal burner's. I could eat nuts and hunt rabbits, now that I know how *not* to cook them. If I stayed in one place long enough, I could soak the peas all day long before I cooked them. The pot is in my pack; the flint and strike-a-light are in my scrip.

John Mouse slows his pace until he walks beside me. "Dreaming, little serving maid?"

How did he know?

"So, they don't dream," he says when I don't answer. "You were only considering what a fine brewet you'll cook for us and the best way to get that stain out of your mistress's cloak."

I hadn't noticed the stain. "I wasn't always a servant," I say.

"No?"

I shake my head. There are so many things I would like to say to John Mouse, but nothing comes to me now. What a simpleton I am.

"Do girls who weren't always servants have names?"

"I'm Johanna."

"Johanna! Then we have the same name day, from St. John the Evangelist."

"I know that." How stupid does he think I am? Very, considering what I've said to him so far. "I was dreaming of running away to the woods and never fixing another meal for certain people."

"Certain people, eh?" He smiles. "I thought yours looked like the face of one who dreams. But beware—as the poet says, 'Dreams, dreams, they mock us with their flitting shadows.'" He winks at me and sprints ahead to rejoin Thomas.

My face looks like the face of one who dreams? We share a name day! My feet no longer hurt. I repeat the poet's words to myself so I won't forget them. "Dreams, dreams, they mock us with their flitting shadows."

John Mouse's words sustain me like a hot eel pie on a cold day. I think of them that evening when Petrus Tappester yells at me for burning the brewet and the next morning when my mistress calls me a wretched girl for poking her when I'm pinning up her headdress. She's lucky I didn't poke any harder.

When Dame Isabel looks down her thin nose at the rip in the bodice of my gown, I run the poet's words over my tongue. They soothe like clear stream water.

I repeat them to myself as we walk so I won't have to hear people bickering, especially my mistress and Petrus Tappester. Even Dame Isabel argues with my mistress, when she's not too busy arguing with her husband.

One cold day, we come to a town where an English-speaking priest tells us that with such discord in our company, we will come to harm unless we have great grace. My mistress follows him into a church. When she comes back to the hospice, she says, "The Lord spoke to me in my mind. He said, 'Don't be afraid, daughter. Your party will come to no harm as long as you are with them.'"

Petrus laughs loudly. Over in the corner, I see Bartilmew moving his lips in prayer.

He does well to pray as long as I am in charge of the cooking.

When I pray, it's to St. Margaret with her dragon; to St. Pega of the Fens; and to St. Guthlac, her brother, with his long, uncombed hair and his ragged clothes, standing patiently while winged devils assail him. They swarm around him like angry bees, but he just waits for their fury to subside. It's harder for me, but then, I'm not a saint.

We march on, day after day. Far in the distance, I can see smoke on the horizon. The merchant says it's not smoke; it's mountains. He must think we're fools. Even I know what mountains look like, and it's not like smoke.

Sometimes it rains, and sometimes the rain turns to sleet. The flat fields give way to hills that strain my legs. We leave the broad waters of the Rhine and follow what the merchant says is a faster route to Constance. Of course, he's the one who thought he knew the route through the forest, too.

One day we come to a set of hills so high that we climb until nightfall and descend all the next day—only to have to climb again on the following day. I can't see the smudge of smoke on the horizon anymore. Instead, I see high hills around me, some of them with snow on their tops. Rocky places open into broad fields, and goat bells jingle somewhere nearby.

While I'm looking around for the goats, I stumble and the sole splits from the rest of my boot. I sit on a rock and tear yet another strip from my linen shift—my clothes are starting to look like St. Guthlac's. Bartilmew sits beside me and helps me tie my boot together, but I'm not sure how long the repair will last. Already my feet ache with the cold in the mornings, especially when we have to camp outside under clouds and spitting rain.

The next morning, we pause at the top of a hill to rest. Cathedral spires shine in the distance like a vision of heaven.

"That's Constance," the merchant says. "Up ahead there. See the lake?"

"Constance?" Dame Isabel says.

"Constance!" Petrus Tappester says, slapping Father Nicholas on the back.

"Blessed be our heavenly Father," my mistress says, and falls to her knees.

We start walking again, quickly now, our spirits high in anticipation of our arrival.

"Is there an English hospice?" Dame Isabel asks.

"A hospice—what about a cobbler?" Petrus Tappester says.

I look at his boots. They're in worse shape than mine.

"Fresh bread is what I'm looking forward to," Father Nicholas says.

"You take the bread; I'll take the ale," Thomas says, and John Mouse laughs.

"Hate to spoil your fun," the merchant says, stroking his beard, "but we've a long way to go. We'll be lucky if we make it by nightfall tomorrow."

Tomorrow! I had thought we'd be there by midday today. Our pace slackens. The merchant reminds us that he'll leave us in Constance, to spend the winter with his friend. "I don't envy the rest of you, having to cross the Alps. See those mountains in the distance? That's where you'll be when I'm snug before a fire."

I look where he's pointing. Ahead I see cruel-looking peaks covered with snow—the peaks we have to cross. I shake my head. I don't think it's possible.

"But after the Alps, we get to Bolzano," John Mouse says. "And then Thomas and I are off to Bologna, to the university."

I draw in a sharp breath. I'd forgotten.

"And we'll head on to Venice, and from there, the Holy Land!" Father Nicholas says, crossing himself.

The rest of them may be going to the Holy Land, but my mistress and I will head to Assisi, where St. Francis preached to the birds, and then to Rome. Without John Mouse.

I watch as he and Thomas have a long conversation, gesticulating at each other, looking grave and then laughing. What do these scholars talk about amongst themselves?

Constance. We finally arrive, my boot now in tatters. The merchant bids us farewell and points us toward the hospice. I want to tell his packhorse goodbye, but the merchant hurries down the crowded street without a backward glance, pulling his horse along with him. Besides, I don't think his horse will miss me as much as he ought to.

On the first morning, my mistress and I go with Petrus Tappester to get our boots repaired. A broad-shouldered cobbler stands up behind a counter when we approach the stall. My mistress and I glance at each other, our eyebrows high with surprise: the cobbler is a woman.

Petrus pushes his way past us to be first, but the cobbler shakes her head and points to me. I grin and pull off my boot, hopping on one foot while she turns it over in her calloused hands. It doesn't take much hammering and needlework before she gives it back to me, ready to wear.

When Petrus steps up to the counter for a second time, the cobbler shakes her head at him again and points at my other boot. When I hold up my foot to show her that it needs no repair, she gestures that I should give it to her anyway.

"God's blood! I'll find a real cobbler, none of this woman pretending she knows what she's doing," Petrus says, and stamps away. The cobbler looks up to watch him go and says something I can't understand. Her mouth curves in a crooked smile.

When she gives my boot back to me, I pull it on and realize it doesn't mash my toes the way it used to. I don't know what she did, but I like it. I try to thank her but I don't know how, and, anyway, she's already gesturing for my mistress to hand over her boots.

As we leave the stall, I see Petrus elbowing his way toward us. He runs into a man carrying an armload of wood who yells something, but Petrus ignores him. I fall back behind my mistress as he nears us—when he's as angry as he looks right now, I could end up bruised.

"Not another cobbler in sight," he says between gritted teeth. "What do these foreigners know, anyway?"

My mistress and I don't wait for him. Now I understand the cobbler's crooked smile when Petrus left—she must have known he'd be back.

All the way back to the hospice, I want to dance, my boots feel so good to my feet. When my mistress gives me a sharp look, I realize I *am* dancing. I stop, but I still can't help myself—every third step, I give a little skip.

Back at the hospice, I sit in front of the fire and stretch my toes toward it, admiring my boots. I'm lost in a summery daydream when a noise beside me makes me jump.

John Mouse stands next to me, a shirt in his hands. He shrugs apologetically and says, "I tore it."

His face looks so comical, like he's a little boy who's stolen a tart, that I laugh. "Shall I fix it for you?"

"Would you?"

I nod, and as he hands me the shirt, his fingers touch mine. I pull my hand back as if I've been burned.

Then he's out of the room, calling for Thomas, and I'm relieved when I hear their voices growing faint as they leave the hospice, because I wouldn't want them to see me blushing so furiously.

As I sew, I try not to imagine the shirt touching John Mouse's bare skin. Instead, I think of his long, elegant fingers, the ones that touched mine. His hands are as soft as a gentlewoman's, supple as a lute player's. Only the ink stains on his fingers mark him for a scholar. No one would ever mistake my hands for a gentlewoman's—they look more like the cobbler's. My nails are dirty and broken, and my fingers are red and rough from hauling wood and water, from making fires and washing linens. Could he feel all that when our fingers met?

I picture John Mouse lifting his long fingers to brush a lock of brown hair from his eyes, the way he does. I picture him covering his eyes with his hands in the middle of a disputation with Thomas, when he is deep in thought, then looking up from them again when he is ready to speak.

I know I shouldn't allow myself these sinful thoughts, but I can't help it. I whisper a quick prayer, but even as I do, I see John's eyes and feel once again the touch of his fingers on mine.

When I finish, I fold the shirt carefully and place it beside the fire so it will be warm when he's ready to put it on.

At the midday meal, John Mouse and Thomas are still off somewhere, but most of the others are already seated. My mistress comes through the doorway all puffed up with pride, a brown-robed friar following her. She shoos Father Nicholas out of the place of honor and sits the friar down. "He's a master of divinity," she says. "And a legate to the Pope himself!"

Dame Isabel sits up a little straighter and nudges her husband to do the same. So does Father Nicholas. I smooth my apron and step into the kitchen for the bread.

There isn't much talk at first. Instead, everyone watches the friar and sends food down the table to him. But after the meal is over, Petrus Tappester squares his shoulders and speaks. "Sir, I don't know what lies she's told you, but we can't have this woman in our company anymore, not while she won't eat meat. We have to go out of our way to find food for her. But you, sir, you could order her to eat meat again."

"And her holy stories," Dame Isabel says, her voice low at first but gathering strength as the friar looks at her. "She acts as if she's a priest, but we all know women aren't allowed to preach."

"Could you tell her not to weep, sir?" her husband asks.

Surely they shouldn't speak to the friar this way. I wish John Mouse were here to say something.

Father Nicholas clears his throat. "I do fear her holy stories will bring us to harm, will cause some to think she is a false Lollard and imprison us all for heresy." He keeps his face down, but I can see his pale eyelids fluttering.

"We sacrifice a great deal for her," Dame Isabel says. "She's never thanked us, not once."

The friar looks first at Petrus and then at Dame Isabel. He looks around the table, letting his gaze fall on each person who has spoken. "If one of you had vowed to walk barefoot to the Holy Land, should I make you dispense with that vow because it displeased the other pilgrims?"

No one answers. Everyone except Petrus lowers their faces.

The friar speaks again. "Dame Margery vowed to abstain from eating meat. As long as the Lord gives her the strength to abstain, I certainly won't order her to eat it. Her weeping? A gift of the Holy Spirit. I have no power over it. As for her holy stories, I will ask that she stop until she meets people who can appreciate what she has to say."

Petrus bursts out, "You don't have to travel with her. You don't have to hear her bawling every single minute of the day and thinking she's more pious than everybody else. She's not going with us if you don't stop her."

"Couldn't you just speak with her, sir?" Dame Isabel says, and her husband nods encouragingly at the friar.

"You have my answer," the friar says.

"Well, that's it, then. She's out of this company. Agreed?" Petrus looks around the table.

Nobody speaks. Father Nicholas looks like he wants to, but he doesn't. I hold my breath.

"I said, agreed?"

"You're right, Petrus; of course you're right," Dame Isabel says.

"I say yes," her husband adds.

Father Nicholas stares down at the table, his lips moving as if he were praying.

"Then I'll see to it myself that she gets to Rome," the friar says. "Madame? Gather your belongings and let us depart."

I start for the door to get our pack.

"Oh, no, you don't," Petrus Tappester says. He jumps up and grabs my arm. "She stays with us. We signed on as a group with a maidservant—you can't go back on that."

They did? Dame Margery offered me to work for everybody from the very beginning? Petrus tightens his grip.

"You would leave me alone and friendless in a foreign land where they don't even speak English?" my mistress says. "With no one to wash and cook for me?"

"Come, madame. The Lord will provide." The friar goes to her and gently takes her arm in his.

My mistress looks up at him with tears on her cheeks as they leave the inn. She never even looks at me.

I watch her walk through the door, leaving me behind.

Petrus grabs my hair, pulling my head back. He leans his face into mine. I wince at his sour breath and shut my eyes to the snaking veins on his nose.

"Don't you dare try to leave. I'll be watching you." He holds on to me long enough to run his eyes down my body before he shoves me away.

I hold back the tears until I'm in the kitchen. The other

servants look at me without interest and go about their business. I slide my back down the wall and bury my wet face in my arms and knees. I don't know how long I've been crying before I realize Bartilmew is crouched on the floor beside me. I raise my head a little, and he sees my tears.

"Your mistress is a holy woman," he says.

"But what about *me*?" I wail. "What will *I* do?"

He looks at me gravely. "God will watch over you," he says. "And I will watch over you."

It doesn't help. My tears flow as fast as my mistress's.

"Come," Bartilmew says, pulling me to my knees beside him. "The saints help those who ask them."

So right there in the kitchen, with the smell of bacon and smoke wafting around us and the sounds of servants' voices in the background, Bartilmew and I pray. And as we pray, vesper bells begin to ring somewhere near us, as if in answer.

I was a fool. The saints didn't hear my prayers after all.

If I had had any inkling how hard this journey would be, I would have run away the first time my mistress mentioned it. In England, at least there were places I could run away *to*. Here, there are only mountains, and beyond them, more mountains.

Wind whistles around cliffs and makes me pull my hood close to my face as I stumble along, alone with my thoughts. Before we left Constance, Father Nicholas saw my mistress. The friar had found her a guide to help her reach Bolzano, an old man from Devonshire, Father Nicholas said. But I don't know how an old man and a woman can survive this journey alone. What if they don't make it over the mountains? I look up at the craggy peaks surrounding me, blocking out the sun. If I can't find my mistress when we get to Bolzano, how will I ever get home?

Our path suddenly opens onto a wide meadow, still green. As we cross it, goats dance away from us. Beyond the meadow, the way narrows and loose shale makes it hard to climb. I slip and bruise my shin on a rock. Limping along behind the others, I don't realize they've come to a stop until my nose hits Bartilmew's pack.

A lake blocks our way, but someone must have seen us coming, because on the rocky shore, a man readies his boat. He agrees to take us across, negotiating the price with gestures and nods since none of us can understand him.

The boat doesn't seem big enough for all of us, and it tips far more than I would like as I clamber aboard. We all have to sit smashed up against each other. Dame Isabel moves so that she's next to John Mouse, but he stands and guides me into his seat, taking hold of my arm to steady me. It would be easier to be smug if the boat didn't choose that moment to rock, pitching me forward in an unbecoming fashion.

I take my place beside Dame Isabel and hold on to the side of the boat for dear life. But the ride turns out to be smooth, and by the time we've reached the other side, my shin no longer aches as much.

The boatman points us toward a village where we can find food and a barn to sleep in for the night.

The next evening, we're not so lucky. Darkness descends when we're nowhere near a village, and we have to sleep in the open, wrapped in our cloaks, the wind whistling around us and rocks biting into our backs. When I wake, the water I carry in my pig's bladder is frozen. It stays that way all day long and the next day, besides.

Then, the morning after that, Petrus Tappester increases the pace. Dame Isabel and her husband have trouble keeping up. Father Nicholas pleads with Petrus to slow down, but he won't. Finally, the rest of us begin walking more slowly, letting Petrus get far out of sight, even though we all know we should stick together on these paths.

John Mouse becomes our leader over stones and across icy brooks, but he asks Thomas and Father Nicholas for advice about which way to go.

Late in the afternoon, we come to a wide, rushing mountain stream. John Mouse and Thomas search up and down its banks for a good place to cross; there's no sign of Petrus or where he forded it.

John Mouse pokes his staff at stones in the water, then stretches out a foot. He is halfway across when a rock under him wobbles. He struggles like an acrobat balancing on another man's shoulders, then collapses into the icy water, his head striking a rock.

Thomas is in the stream instantly. The water batters his legs, and he slips on stones. He pulls John Mouse's head above water, but I don't see how he'll get him back to shore. I lift my skirts to rush into the water, but Bartilmew pushes me back and wades through the rapids.

Together, he and Thomas drag John Mouse through the water and over the rocks. They heave him onto the bank, where his body lies in a crumpled heap.

"He breathes," Thomas says.

Father Nicholas kneels beside him, praying. I whip off my cloak and lay it over him, whispering a prayer.

"Fire," Bartilmew says.

There's hardly any fuel, just bracken and twigs, but I rush to gather them. My hands shake as I pull out my flints and a few bits of wool, but I get a flame going.

I am spreading wet garments on the stones before the fire when John Mouse groans and opens his eyes.

"Blessed be God," Dame Isabel says, and bursts into tears.

Tears spring to my eyes, too, and I murmur another prayer to the Virgin.

As I watch, John Mouse tries to sit up and quickly lowers his head again, groaning. Thomas leans toward him.

"Thomas. When did you multiply yourself?" John Mouse says, and shuts his eyes.

"How's your head?" Thomas asks.

"Two hundred stonemasons are building a cathedral inside it. All hammering at the same time." He shivers. Although he jests, his voice quavers.

Dame Isabel's eyes widen. She's thinking what I'm thinking, I'm sure—what if he catches a fever?

"Well, amicus, have a master bring those journeymen under control while we dry our clothes. Next time you want a swim, may I suggest summer?"

"It's God's punishment for leaving behind the holy woman," Bartilmew says, the longest speech I have heard him make.

"Nonsense," Dame Isabel's husband says. "It's that fool who went on ahead—it's Petrus Tappester's fault."

"We should thank God we are all alive," Father Nicholas says. He begins to pray. I drop to my knees. So does Bartilmew. Side by side, Dame Isabel and her husband sink to the ground, and Thomas folds his hands in prayer.

When John Mouse can walk, shakily and with the help

of Thomas and Bartilmew, we set out again. Crossing the stream takes us forever, and even after that, our progress is painfully slow. John Mouse sees two stones for every one the rest of us see, and he says the stonemasons inside his head will take no rest. We stop every few steps for him to catch his breath.

A few paces beyond the stream, the path turns sharply. Just after the turn, we come upon a pile of four stones set up like a little tower—a waymark. We pass three more of them as we walk.

"Look!" Thomas calls. We can see a building atop a steep incline, and as the light fades, we hear bells.

We follow the bells, moving more and more slowly as the sky darkens and John Mouse grows weaker.

Three figures appear on the path ahead of us, and as they come toward us out of the darkness, I can make out the shapes of Petrus Tappester and two monks.

Petrus and one of the monks take John Mouse's arms over their shoulders and drag him to the hospice, the building we can see. Here in the midst of the mountains, the other monk tells us, monks have built a place for travelers like us. The brothers who live in the priory have vowed to serve pilgrims. Their infirmarian will look after John Mouse.

I hear Bartilmew mumbling a prayer and Father Nicholas saying one aloud. I add my voice. We all do. Never has a hospice appeared at such a moment of need.

We are treated to warm porridge, which I don't even have to serve. The monks act like I'm a pilgrim, not a servant—I get to sit on a bench and stretch my feet toward the fire while my gown dries. Then they show us to warm beds with plenty of blankets. This is what Heaven must feel like.

In the morning, we go to the chapel to hear Mass. I know I'm not the only one who prays for John Mouse, but I doubt anyone else says a prayer for my mistress. Except maybe Bartilmew.

Then we gather before the fireplace for another meal. While we eat, the monk who speaks English tells us what the infirmarian has said about John Mouse. It will be several days—perhaps weeks—before he can leave.

"If you're to get over the mountains before the snow and avalanches trap you, every day counts," he adds.

"We can't break up our party," Dame Isabel says. "We have to wait for him." I look at her face. When we left Zierikzee, she was pink and fat and healthy. Now her skin is as rough and brown as mine from the sun and wind. Her face looks drawn and frightened. When she speaks, she avoids her husband's gaze.

"We're leaving, and we're doing it today," Petrus Tappester says.

"You'll go without me, then," Thomas says.

"And without me," Dame Isabel says, staring fiercely into the fire.

"My dear," her husband says, but she cuts him off with a wave of her hand.

"We vowed to stay together and help each other. We can't leave without him," she says.

Where was that vow when they kicked my mistress out of the company?

The monk settles the battle for us. We can't all stay here for the winter, he tells us. "You, yes," he says, pointing at Thomas. "But not the rest of you." He says the hospice has to be ready for other travelers in need, so we must move on.

Dame Isabel lowers her head, and as I turn, I see a tear hesitating on the tip of her eyelash.

Tears prick at my eyes, too. Go on without John Mouse? As I gather my pack, the tears spill over. What if I never see him again? I wipe at my nose, but it does no good.

Does he remember that we share a name day? Or the song he turned from Latin into English for me? I touch my arm where he put his hand on it so long ago, when I was sick on the English Sea. Now I know what he meant when he said, "Dreams, dreams, they mock us with their flitting shadows." Dreams I didn't even know I had evaporate as I think of the road ahead, and of John Mouse here in the infirmary without me.

It takes us fifteen more days to reach Bolzano. So says Father Nicholas, although Petrus Tappester argues that it was only fourteen days. Without the warmth of John Mouse's smile, I am too cold to count the days of our misery.

I know that two nights we camped under rocks, and I awoke to find snow on my cloak and my fingers too stiff to build a fire. And that because I couldn't get a fire going the first night, Petrus threatened me.

Bartilmew helped me, showing me how to drop the glowing char-cloth into a bird's nest of kindling so it wouldn't blow out in the wind. The next night that we spent outdoors, my fire caught so quickly that Petrus never had a chance to complain.

The monks told us to follow the path marked by the little towers of stone, which would take us from hospice to village to hospice. If we had followed their advice, Dame Isabel's gown wouldn't have caught on fire.

On one of our nights outside, she got too close to the flames trying to get warm. Bartilmew stamped out her burning gown fast enough that she wasn't burned, but the singed edges make her even more sour than usual.

If she is sour, like an apple eaten too early, Petrus Tappester is as rotten as an apple whose core has been gnawed by a wasp. He's the one who ordered the rest of us to follow him on a trail of his own devising, away from the waymarks. We nearly froze for his folly and spent two nights in the snow.

Our mornings begin with arguments, our dinners are spiced with quarrels, our suppers are served with squabbles like large helpings of thistles. Surely God will never allow Petrus Tappester into the Holy Land after all the things he has said and done. A pilgrimage is supposed to be a kind of penance, but he'll need to do penance for his pilgrimage. We all will. Maybe even me.

Descending is as hard as climbing, except for the knowledge that each step takes us closer to Bolzano, with its warm beds and hot food. Snow and icy rocks begin to give way to scraggly trees, and trees to snow-covered fields. Curls of smoke and crowing roosters signal farms and villages. We sleep in barns, warmed by cows and goats.

One night in a village, everyone sleeps in an inn. I survey the kitchen, trying to find the best place to curl up, when the inn's maidservant, who must be about Cicilly's age and has black braids that shine in the firelight, takes me by the hand and leads me out and down the snowy street. We stop in front of the huge village oven, built right into the mountainside. She opens the door, touches the warm stone, and climbs in, gesturing for me to follow.

There's room for us both, and the heat left over from

the day's baking seeps into my back, my legs, my aching bones. The smell of warm bread envelops me. In sleep, I am home with Rose on her baking days and the warmth of our garden in summer.

Just as light begins to seep around the door's edges, an old woman with eyes deep in her wrinkled face shoos us out, but she smiles and gives us each a hunk of barley bread that she has tied up in her apron. We race back to the inn.

After a warm night and kind strangers, I find my way over the rocks easily all day long, my head full of the sound of John Mouse's laughter, the sight of him winking at me.

Then, after fifteen days, or fourteen if you believe Petrus Tappester, we arrive at the hospice in Bolzano.

My mistress isn't there.

"Too soon," Bartilmew says when he sees me looking through the dormitory. "Wait."

That's what he says, but what if she's lost in the snow somewhere? What if she has fallen down a cliff or been overtaken by robbers? What if the mercenaries found her? I pray to St. Margaret to keep her safe.

When I go back to the common room, a pile of clothes greets me. "Those need to be washed," Dame Isabel says. "And some need mending."

"Where's our supper? Hurry up, girl," Petrus says.

I want to kick the pile of clothes and storm out of the hospice. Don't they think I get tired? Don't they know how hungry and cold I am?

I stomp into the kitchen to find the sack of meal allotted to us. Inside the sack, something's moving. I look closer—weevils, hundreds of them, crawling through the barley meal. Ugh. There are far too many for me to pick them out. I shut the sack and stare at it for a moment. Then I dump the meal into a pot of water and hang it over the fire.

Once it's boiled, they'll never notice. At least, I hope not.

While it cooks, I scrounge around for my own supper, scraping the moldy edge off a piece of hard cheese I've been carrying for weeks and digging deep in my pack for an oatcake.

When I serve the bowls, Petrus Tappester and Dame Isabel are arguing about how long we should stay in Bolzano. They never look at their food, just spoon it into their mouths. Father Nicholas blinks at his for a minute. Then he stirs it and starts eating.

I feel bad about Bartilmew—but not bad enough to say anything. And, anyway, for all I know, weevils might taste fine.

After supper, it's too dark out to wash clothes, and besides, they'd never dry. They can wait till morning. In the kitchen, I find a place near the fire and hunch over Dame Isabel's husband's hose, trying to mend the rip in them. My fingers are so rough they snag the wool, and I jab myself with the needle. Blood speckles my skirt and the hose.

Finally, I finish, my seams a crazy zigzag. Cook would laugh if she could see them. I toss the hose on the pile of laundry and stand, stretching and rubbing at the place on my neck that's sore from leaning over my mending. I'm going to bed.

A voice stops me, low and dangerous. "I thought I told you to wash my clothes," Petrus Tappester says.

"I will. In the morning. It's too dark for them to dry now."

I see his hand just before it hits me.

My fingers fly to the side of my head.

"Put them in front of the fire, stupid girl. They'll dry." He stalks out.

I stand there, shaking with fury. I hate him so much.

Where does he think I'm going to do all this washing, when I don't know my way around and it's dark out?

I probe my head and feel a lump. I hope the devil finds Petrus Tappester.

A log rolls over in the fire, making the flames leap. I look toward the room's shadowy corners where devils sometimes hide. Did something move? I cross myself.

Quickly, I paw through the clothes to find Petrus's breeches, then slip out the hospice door. For a moment, I stand in the dark, letting my eyes get accustomed to the pale moonlight. The stable looms ahead of me. I stumble toward it, bruising my toes on stones.

Inside the stable it's even darker, and I have to feel my way forward until I find the horses' trough, the water crusted with ice. I bunch Petrus's breeches around my hand and punch through it. Bits of oats and hay float in the water, and horses have slobbered in it, but I don't care.

I pound the breeches against the side of the trough to loosen the dirt, then plunge them back into the water. When I yank them back out again, the cloth catches on something. I pull again but nothing happens. I pull harder.

Suddenly, the breeches are in my hands, and I have to step back to steady myself.

I wring them out and rush, shivering madly, back into the kitchen. When I spread the breeches on the bench before the fire, I see the huge rip.

I can't stop my tears. I kick at the bench. All I want to do is sleep, but now these loathsome breeches. If I don't fix them, Petrus might really hurt me.

I wish John Mouse were here now. Oh, Cook, oh, Cicilly, oh, Rose.

I collapse in a crumpled heap before the fire, the wet, ripped breeches in my hands.

The sound of a rooster crowing draws me from a hazy dream. It's dark and the fire has died out, but I can hear a horse clopping past, a woman clucking at hens, the bleating of sheep. Morning sounds. I start to stand and then stop as I sway, my hand to the lump on my head. When the dizziness passes, I stand again, more slowly this time.

Petrus's damp breeches fall out of my lap, where they've left a wet spot on my skirt, and land on the dirt floor.

I stare at them.

Somewhere nearby, church bells are tolling.

I listen, but I hear no sounds from the hospice. No one is up. Silently, I glide out the door. I look up the narrow street, then down it, until I find the bell tower.

Grabbing my skirts, I walk quickly, glancing behind me every few steps. In a church, at Mass, Petrus Tappester wouldn't dare touch me.

Three widows in black dresses climb the steps to the church door. I follow them in and find a place beside a column where I can kneel to pray.

I'm in the midst of a prayer to St. Pega and her brother, St. Guthlac, when a sound makes me catch my breath.

"Ah, sweet Jesu," a voice cries out. A sob follows.

My mistress has made it over the mountains.

I feel a weight lifting from me, as if I had just taken off my pack. I look through the dark church until I find my mistress kneeling among a group of women, her eyes closed in prayer.

I redouble my own prayers. The Lord has been merciful to us both.

When Mass is over, I follow Dame Margery out, marveling at how white her gown is. It's new, not the one that Petrus Tappester ripped the bottom off of, the one that was filthy from weeks of mud and rain and wading through streams.

She walks with three very fine ladies—they're so fine that I'm afraid to approach them.

"Dame Margery," I call.

She turns. Her wimple is well-pinned, her veil beautifully starched. How did she do that without me?

She frowns. With an impatient gesture, she signals me to follow.

I stay a few steps back. I can hear the ladies' gowns rustling like summer oaks. Is it silk that sounds so rich?

When we come to a tall building with broad steps lead-ing up to a massive wooden door, like a church, Dame Margery hisses, "Go around to the kitchen." The door opens and she and the ladies disappear through it.

I walk around the house, gazing up at the high stone walls, my mouth open. A boy looks down at me from a window, then draws his head back in. When I find a low door in the back, I peer through. The kitchen.

When I step inside, a man standing by the fireplace speaks to me, but I can't understand him. His dark hair surrounds his face in tight curls, and a thin mustache curves like a caterpillar on his lip. I've never seen anything like it before.

His voice gets louder and he gestures at me, but I still can't understand.

When he speaks again, his voice is angry. He rushes at me as if I were a goose, chasing me away.

I stumble backward, outside. The door slams shut.

What do I do now? My mistress won't be able to find me, and I don't speak the language.

I wander back to the front of the house. I don't think they'd like it if I knocked.

I lower myself onto the steps. My stomach growls and my head aches where Petrus hit me, but I'd rather wait here than back at the hospice.

Between two buildings, the sun peers from behind a cloud, climbing into morning. A dove lands on the street with a whooshing noise and pecks at a clump of dirt. Somewhere nearby, hooves clop, coming toward me. I watch as a mule appears from around the corner, a basket on either side of its back, a shabbily dressed man hitting it with a stick. The man sees me, then shakes his head quickly, giving me some kind of message as he goes past. What does he mean?

The door opens and I jump up.

A man in a fine black robe and a sort of turban on his head comes out, pulling on gloves. Behind him comes a younger man, this one in a bright blue tunic and red hose.

I drop a little curtsy. "Beg pardon, I'm looking for Dame Margery."

They stare at me. Then the younger man shoos at me the same way the man in the kitchen did. Can't they see I'm not a chicken?

"Dame Margery," I say more loudly, drawing out the words, so they'll understand. "Mar-ger-y Kempe."

The two men speak to each other rapidly. Then the younger one goes to the door and shouts something.

Finally. I smooth my skirt and wait for my mistress, keeping my eyes down so the men won't think I'm too forward.

A huge man comes out, tall and brawny, even bigger than Petrus Tappester. I shift to see if Dame Margery is behind him. He keeps coming, directly toward me.

Before I can step out of the way, the man lifts me up and carries me down the steps.

"Stop! Put me down!" I yell. I crane my neck back to see my mistress, but she's not there.

The man keeps going. The more I squirm, the tighter he grips me. "Let me go! Help!" I call to two young men walking down the street.

They laugh and keep walking.

When we get to the corner, the man drops me. In the mud.

When I look up, he's halfway back to the house again. I stand, brushing at my cloak, rubbing my backside where I landed and my elbow where it hit the ground. Angry tears blur my sight as I stare back at the house.

Where is my mistress?

There's nothing for me to do but go back to the hospice. Back to where I left Petrus Tappester's torn breeches and a pile of unwashed laundry.

I creep down the street, past the church, and toward the hospice. When I stop at the door, I can't hear anybody, or see them, either, so I tiptoe in. The pile of clothes lies on the floor where I left it, Petrus's breeches on top. I grab them all.

Down the street the opposite way, I see a well. As I near it, I watch two girls Rose's age talking and laughing as they pound clothes against the stone sides of the holding tank. When I approach, they stare at me. "Benedicite," I say, crossing myself—I don't want them to shoo me off, too.

One of them says something, but I shake my head to show her I can't understand. She shrugs and goes back to her washing and her chatter.

As I immerse Dame Isabel's gown into the cold water, I see them eyeing me, but they keep talking to each other. Before long, it's as if I'm not even there.

After I've washed the pile of clothes, I tackle my cloak, shivering in the chill breeze while I scrub the mud off it. If it wasn't so cold, I'd stay here to mend Petrus's breeches, too, but I can't thread the needle when my hands shake so much.

When I get near the hospice, I hear voices. As I drape damp clothing over a low wall by the hospice door, I listen. My mistress is here.

"God willed it," she's saying. "How else could I have made it here two days before you did?"

That's easy: She didn't have Petrus Tappester leading her astray. When I finish hanging out the clothes, I hover by the door.

Someone says something, Father Nicholas, I think, but I can't make it out. But I can certainly hear Dame Margery.

"Dona Caterina invited me to stay at her house. She knows Brother Alphonse, the friar I met in Constance— the one who presented me with this fine gown."

I peek in to see her preening in front of Dame Isabel and Father Nicholas. When I see Petrus Tappester scowling at her from a corner, I duck out, my heart pounding.

"I'm not listening to this," he says. "Don't think you're going to Venice with us, not with all your crying and your holy talk."

I hear his boots hitting the ground hard as he comes toward the door. Where can I go? There's no place for me to hide. I lower my face and look at the ground.

He stomps past me without a word.

As he turns a corner, I let out my breath.

The moment I come through the door, my mistress sees me. "And you," she says, her eyes narrowed in anger, "you wretched girl, leaving me all alone like that."

"No, mistress, you don't understand, they—"

"I understand wickedness when I see it," she says.

"But I went to the kitchen; they wouldn't let me in."

She slaps my face. I step back, dazed.

"You left me to cross the Alps alone with just an old man to see to my needs," she says.

I left her?

"I'll be at Dona Caterina's," Dame Margery says to the others. She turns back to me. "And I certainly don't need you there. Dona Caterina has lent me her own personal maid while I'm in Bolzano." She sweeps out of the hospice.

21

i may doubt my mistress's holiness right now, my cheek still burning from the slap she gave me, but Dame Isabel doesn't. Not anymore. "The Lord saw her over the mountains, and he'll see her to Venice, too," she says. "We need her in our company."

Her husband nods, and Father Nicholas is quick to agree.

"You must go to Dona Caterina's house and beg her to come with us," Dame Isabel tells the priest.

"That's all fine to say, but what about Petrus?" her husband says. "He'll never agree to it."

"Petrus isn't the only one on this pilgrimage," Dame Isabel says, stretching herself tall. "I'll speak to him."

By the time I serve supper, it's official. My mistress will rejoin the company. Until we leave, she's staying at Dona Caterina's—without me.

"You mark me," Petrus says, waving his bread toward Dame Isabel. "One word out of her and it's over."

"Now, Petrus," Dame Isabel says. "I'm sure there will be no trouble."

The trouble comes two days later when Petrus decides it's time to leave Bolzano.

"Certainly not," Dame Isabel says. "We've barely arrived." She flicks her eyes toward the door.

I do, too. We're both waiting for John Mouse and Thomas. If my mistress made it over the mountains so quickly, they could, too. They could be here any minute. If we leave without them, I'll never see them again—they go straight from here to the university at Bologna.

Like Dame Isabel, I'm content to stay in this hospice as long as we can, even if it does mean my keeping to corners and out-of-the-way places where Petrus won't find me. I mended his breeches, but the seams look like crooked scars. I put them on the bottom of the pile of clothes in a dark corner. So far he hasn't said anything.

In fact, nobody pays any attention to me unless they want something. Except Bartilmew. He gives me nods of acknowledgment or looks of commiseration when Petrus shouts at me.

In the end, Petrus prevails. Five days have passed with no sign of the students, and he says we have to leave. I watch behind me all the way out of town, but I catch no sight of them.

The trip to Venice is the easiest we have had so far. We sail down rivers, never out of sight of land, and when I stand on deck and look out at the horizon, the queasy feeling leaves my stomach. In its place is a huge emptiness for John Mouse.

As the mountains recede, I think of him in the infirmary, high in the Alps, and pray for him.

*　*　*

The strange city of water welcomes us. As we disembark, men rush up to us saying, "Deutsch? Français? English?" A short, wiry man with a stooped back attaches himself to us and hurries us off the quay.

"Good place to stay, clean, cheap," he says. "For you English, good cheap."

He leads us, pulling at our arms, pushing Dame Isabel's husband from behind, and making us laugh. We go through narrow streets, over bridges, around corners, past churches. It's so bright, with orange roofs and paintings on the walls and buildings so big they make the guildhall in Lynn look like a toy. There's water everywhere, more water even than in Lynn. People rush past, ladies carried in litters, tradesmen leading donkeys, boys in rich tunics, and boys in beggars' rags. Everywhere, tippy-looking boats ply the waters.

We pass shops and market stalls: money changers, tailors, cobblers, rope sellers, cloth dealers waving bright fabrics. Wondrous smells prick at my nose—spices and sizzling meats and something sweet, I don't know what. Men reach out to us, holding fruits and fowls and long loaves of bread. I'm dizzy with the colors and noises and smells, but our guide leads us too quickly for me to stop and look.

He takes us down a dark alley so narrow that when I reach out, my fingers brush against the walls on both sides. When we finally stop, it's in front of a two-story building whose windows have no shutters.

"You have servants? Better that way," the guide says. "Good price for you English," he says before he and Petrus start bickering. They come to an agreement and shake hands.

When the guide leaves, Dame Isabel, her husband, and Dame Margery all turn on Petrus. "That's the best you could do?" Dame Isabel says.

"We haven't even looked inside," her husband adds.

"I'm not paying that much," Dame Margery says. "I won't be here long, anyway—I'll be leaving for Assisi."

"You'll pay the same as the rest of us," Petrus tells her.

I close my ears and look through the door, which hangs drunkenly on one hinge. When I step in, the smell is terrible. Dame Isabel's husband was right.

Someone must have kept chickens here, because the floor is covered with white droppings. In the corners, damp hay and who knows what else rots in piles. I wrinkle my nose. I'm glad my mistress and I are leaving soon. Poor Bartilmew. He'll have to stay here till spring when the ships leave for the Holy Land. He has a long wait.

Upstairs smells a little better, but the stairs creak ominously, as if I might fall right through them. No poultry have bedded down up here, and there's no moldy hay. Neither is there any furniture, not even a cot. The Venetian must be back down on the wharf having a good laugh with his friends.

In the afternoon, my mistress decides to visit a convent Dona Caterina told her about. "Come along, girl," she says.

I follow her through the strange streets, my eyes wide

with the sights. We pass a market and cross bridge after bridge.

Dame Margery stops at a fork in the road, closes her eyes, moves her lips, and nods. "The Lord tells me it's this way," she says, and starts up again.

The Lord knows his directions. In almost no time at all, we arrive at the convent gate.

My mistress rings a bell. When a small door in the wall opens, she pushes through her letter from Dona Caterina. I can hear women's voices. Then the door swings open, and two nuns usher us in. I don't know what it says in that letter, but the nuns greet my mistress like she's their lost pet lamb, smiling and saying all sorts of things we can't understand. They take us across a dusty courtyard and into a chapel, where my mistress kneels before a statue of the Virgin.

Oh, no. I can see it coming.

She screws up her face and lets out a howling sob. I wince and glance around me nervously. But the nuns approve. They raise my mistress up and walk her slowly out of the chapel, tears streaming down her cheeks. Across the courtyard, we go into a richly appointed chamber. I slip in just before the door shuts.

The nun awaiting my mistress must be the abbess. A jeweled cross around her neck sparkles in the firelight when she comes forward to kiss my mistress's cheeks. She says something, and the other nuns help my mistress into a cushioned chair. When a servant enters with a tray, they offer her dainty cakes of some kind. My mistress chews, tears running into her mouth, while the nuns chatter.

When the jeweled nun says something, they take the tray away and all of them kneel. My mistress slips off her chair and onto her knees. I kneel, too.

We begin with the Ave Maria, although the words sound so funny the way the nuns say them that it takes me a while to recognize it. Then the Paternoster, and then some other prayers I don't know.

We pray for a long time. When the nuns stand, my mistress remains on her knees, tears flowing. At least they're silent tears this time.

From under lowered lashes, I watch the nuns nodding and smiling at each other. They may be happy now, but they don't know how lucky they are that we're going to Assisi soon.

When we leave, they pet me, too, their soft hands like feathers on my shoulders and arms.

Back at our hostel, I wish we could have stayed at the convent. I spend the rest of the day trying to clean the stinking piles of dung and hay and chicken droppings from the floor, and then cooking some kind of grain that Dame Isabel and her husband bought at the market. I boil it as long as I can, adding water every time it boils away, but the grain never softens. It might as well be peas. Everyone grumbles when they try to eat it, and I don't blame them. At least no one breaks a tooth.

In the morning, they send me to find bread and cheese. All by myself. I wish Bartilmew could come along, but Dame Isabel has him cleaning out the room she and her husband are sharing.

In the street, two men pass me, speaking loudly in a

foreign language. I shrink back against a wall and let them pass. When they're gone, I step into the street again. A sunbeam slants between buildings, cheering me. I head for the market my mistress and I passed on the way to the convent.

I cross over a canal, go past an alley, and peer around a corner where I'm sure the market is—but it's not there. Was it the other direction? I can't remember. And what will I do when I get there? I don't know how much anything costs. I don't even know how much the coin Dame Isabel gave me is worth. I open my hand and look at the face on it.

Just as I do, someone bumps into me, hard.

"*Scusi, scusi,*" a boy says, backing away from me. His clothes are in rags, but he's grinning. Then another ragged boy runs around the corner, saying something to the first. They laugh and, looking back at me, run down a dark alley.

Suddenly, I realize the coin is gone.

"Thieves!" I shout, and take off down the alley after them. Where are they? I pound down the alley, holding up my skirts so I don't trip. The farther I go, the more crowded the alley gets. I catch sight of one boy, but then he disappears behind two women and melts into the crowd.

When I realize how many people are watching me, I slow my pace. A woman with a painted face leers up at me from a doorstep. A man steps forward and grasps my cloak.

"Let go!" I say.

He laughs.

A woman says something behind me. I whirl. She smiles, showing her missing front teeth.

When she plucks at my gown, I start running back the way I came.

The man who grabbed my cloak chases me, his boots slapping the ground.

My breath coming in sharp gasps, I push my way between startled people, running with all my might.

The footsteps die away behind me, and I can hear the man laughing, but I keep going.

Finally, I emerge from the alley. Panting, I look behind me, but no one's following me.

There's nothing I can do. The coin is gone.

I look to the right and then to the left. Which way? I know I crossed a canal—this one? I go over the bridge and down a street. Voices and bright colored fabrics tell me I've come to the very market I was trying to find. Loaves of bread are stacked high in one stall, and when I look behind me, I see great wheels of cheese. But now I have no way to buy them.

I don't know what I'll say to Dame Isabel. What will Petrus do to me this time? There's no point in hurrying back. The market swirls around me, voices and laughter, the smell of cooking meat, the sound of a dog barking.

I lower myself onto a set of steps and watch a boy juggling four red and yellow balls. The hat in front of him is as empty of coins as my hands are. He gives me a sad little smile, then looks back at the balls he's juggling.

Finally, I turn back toward the hostel. Twice, I take a wrong turn and have to retrace my steps. Even though I'm afraid of Petrus, I'm relieved when I finally see our hostel. I pick up my pace.

Bartilmew greets me at the door, a wild look in his eye. "She left. For Assisi," he says, the sounds making spit fly from his mouth.

I shake my head, not comprehending.

"Your mistress," he says. "She's gone."

22

my mistress is gone?

"I have to find her. Where's my pack?" I push past Bartilmew, but he grabs my shoulders.

"Johanna," he says. It's the first time I've heard my name in weeks. I look at him.

"She took the pack." Every word is difficult for him, but he keeps talking. "After you left. I tried to find you."

"I'll catch up with her. Which way did she go?" My body is ready to keep running.

"She's on a boat," he says. "Gone."

Gone? This time the word sinks in, sounding like a funeral bell.

Suddenly, I'm so tired my whole body slumps. If it weren't for Bartilmew catching my elbow, I'd fall. He walks me inside. I lean against the wall, then slide down it until I'm crouching on the floor, my knees to my chest.

What will I do? How will I find her? How will I ever get home now?

Bartilmew lays his huge hand on top of my head, the

warmth of it spreading through me. As he walks away, my tears begin.

I don't know how long I've been there when something touches my foot. I look up, my eyes swollen. Dame Isabel prods me with her shoe.

"Where's the bread you bought?" she asks.

I shake my head. Things can't get any worse. I might as well tell her. "Stolen," I say, my voice a harsh croak.

"What do you mean, stolen?" she says, as if that's impossible. "Where is it?"

"Somebody stole the coin."

She stares at me, her mouth an oval. "My money!" she shrieks. "Husband! Where are you? Petrus! Come here!"

I close my eyes and lower my head to my knees. The cold of the wall seeps into my back.

In my bones, I feel the vibrations as someone comes down the wooden stairs.

"What's this racket?" Petrus says.

I retreat further into the dark behind my eyelids.

"The money we gave her for bread and cheese. Stolen, or so she says," Dame Isabel says. "I knew we couldn't trust her."

"Who stole it?" Petrus says.

"Ask *her*," Dame Isabel says. "She's the one who had it last."

I can feel her pointing at me, but I dare not raise my head. I tense for Petrus's blows, not knowing where they will fall. I hear him kick a wall and grunt. Then his footsteps recede.

"*Do* something!" Dame Isabel shrieks. Her footsteps follow his, and then I hear her husband going after her.

"There, now, my honey bird," he says.

Then they are gone. In the silence, I whisper an Ave. And then another and another.

More footsteps. I tense.

Someone crouches in front of me.

Bartilmew.

He unfurls my fist and fills it with bread. Turning his head toward the door and then back to me, he gestures toward his mouth.

I don't know where he got it. It's so old and dry that it's hard to swallow, but I chew until I can get it down.

Bartilmew stands and reaches his hand toward mine. I take it and let him haul me up. Together, we return to the work of cleaning the piles of rotten hay and chicken droppings from the floor.

Slowly, the day passes. Every time I start to think about what will happen to me, I stop myself.

Dame Isabel's husband comes in with a cooking pot for me to use, now that my mistress has taken the old one. He also brings barley meal, which I cook to perfection—no lumps, no burning, just smooth porridge. Still, it tastes terrible because my mistress took the salt.

As I serve them, I watch Dame Isabel and Petrus nervously, waiting for my punishment for the stolen coin. No one says anything about it, which makes me more nervous. What are they waiting for?

When night comes, I wrap myself in my cloak and try

to sleep. My hood was in the pack that my mistress took. So was my blanket. I shiver in the dark, and my thoughts fly around me like St. Guthlac's winged demons, tempting me to despair.

How will I ever find my mistress again? How will I get back home? I don't know how long Dame Isabel will let me stay here, especially since she thinks I was the one who stole the coin. I can't go with them to the Holy Land—I have no way to pay for my passage on the ship they'll take. What will I do when they're gone?

My fears whirl me into a stupor until I finally fall into dark dreams.

Each day I awake afraid. As much as I hate and fear Petrus Tappester, as little love as I hold for Dame Isabel and her husband, I do their bidding as well as I can. My next mistake might be my last in their company.

When Petrus slaps me, I bear it without tears, except when it hurts so much I can't help it. When Dame Isabel calls me "sullen child" or "wicked girl," I ignore her words. She's like a demon, tempting me to anger, but I clench my fists and keep my face as expressionless as I can. If I give in, they could kick me out.

Father Nicholas never calls me names or hits me, but he doesn't defend me, either. Instead, he pretends not to see or hurries away when the shouting starts. He's found a church where he spends his time doing I don't know what. Not studying the Gospels, surely, or wouldn't he be raising up the weak? Me, I mean?

* * *

One cold, sunny day, Petrus goes out in the morning and doesn't come back in time for the midday meal. I feel lighter than I have for days. After we eat, Dame Isabel and her husband go out to see some of Venice's sights, and Father Nicholas slips away to his church.

I take the pot out to the nearest canal to wash it and bring it back full of water. The sky is a cold and cloudless blue, as bright and clean as new milk. I set the pot down and watch a seagull hovering on the wind. Down one street, a white sheet drying on a line strung between buildings billows in the breeze like a sail.

In the distance, I can hear someone singing. Another voice joins in. It's a happy song, whatever they sing, and it makes me think of John Mouse and remember the time we sang together, just for a moment, before the others joined in.

When the voices die out, I pick up my pot again, sloshing water over my boots. I don't even care.

Back at our hostel, I come through the door, blinking in the gloom. As I set the pot down, I hear something behind me.

"Bartilmew?" I say.

Hands grab me. One clamps over my mouth. A body presses into mine. I feel the cold touch of iron at my neck. My heart pounds in my throat.

"Not a word out of you, girl, or you'll feel more of this knife," Petrus says. His words stink of stale wine.

I try to wrench myself away, but the knife bites into my neck, just below my ear. He's too strong for me.

"Nobody here, just you and me," he says, pulling me back with him, away from the door.

His fingers mash my lips against my teeth. As he pulls me back, his fingers spread. I bite down, hard.

"Damn you!" He pulls his hand away.

I scream. His hand covers my mouth again, tight and hard.

I struggle, but I can't get away. The knife starts to cut. Far away I can see a bright blue box, the sky through the door.

He backs toward the stairs, pulling me with him.

I hear a growl, then footsteps.

I stumble, and Petrus jerks me upright, his meaty fingers grasping my neck, crushing it. I can't breathe.

"Johanna! Run!"

Bartilmew's voice.

I scratch at Petrus's arm, trying to wriggle away from him, but the hand on my neck tightens.

"Oof!" Petrus says, and suddenly, I'm free. I scramble out of his grip.

"Go!" Bartilmew bellows.

Tripping over my skirt, I stumble toward the blue box.

I push through the door and over the threshold.

I look back. Bartilmew and Petrus are locked in a fighter's embrace, the knife raised high.

As I flee, the knife comes down.

Blindly, I run, a scream stifled in my throat.

Through the alley, down a narrow street, past a church, through the empty marketplace, the stalls closed for the day. Across a bridge, along a narrow canal side path, across another bridge.

I push past a group of boys and break through a man and a woman walking arm in arm. The man shouts, but I keep running.

I run until the sharp pain in my side makes me stop. I lean against a wall, holding my ribs and gasping for air.

When I can breathe again, I touch my neck. The blood on my fingers makes me look down—there's blood on my cloak, too.

A sound makes me whirl, but it's nothing, just a man walking past in a hurry. I look around me. I'm in an open area, the largest space I've seen in Venice that isn't the sea.

Two young men stare at me as they go by.

I can't stay here. I start walking. I walk all afternoon and longer, until the sky turns the brilliant blue of a winter twilight, until a star pierces it, until the blue fades to gray.

I don't know where I'm going, just that I have to keep walking.

The scent of incense on the breeze tells me a church is nearby. When I find it, I look around furtively before creeping through the door. I don't think anyone sees me.

A few candles up by the altar are the only light. I stumble through the shadows until I find a corner where I can lower myself to the floor and rest my trembling legs. When I'm sure no one has seen me, I wrap myself tightly in my cloak to wait out the night, wishing I had my hood.

Now that my body has stopped moving, my mind races. Over and over again I see Bartilmew and Petrus, close as two dancers, their arms raised, the knife coming down. Who held it? I couldn't see.

I close my eyes as tightly as I can and rub them with the heels of my hands to make the image go away, but I can't stop seeing it.

I should have stayed. I should have helped Bartilmew. What happened to him? Is he all right?

I should pray for him, but no prayer comes. Instead, anger flares inside me. This is all Dame Margery's fault. How could she leave me all alone in a foreign land? How *could* she?

My breathing slows and a calm takes over me, a quiet, steady flame of anger that fills me.

From far away, the sound of chimes awakens me. I blink in the dim light and listen, trying to understand where I am.

The chimes ring again, and I realize they're not so far

away after all: Up at the altar, acolytes ring bells as the priests chant Mass. In the dark nave, ghostly figures kneel in prayer. Something catches my eye, making me look up. A sparrow flits through the roofbeams and lands near a stained-glass window. I squint until I can see the image: St. Michael holding his scales.

I rise slowly and make my way through the church. As I get closer to the altar, the smell of incense wafts past me. It catches in my throat and makes my stomach heave.

My hand over my mouth, I run through the nave, out the church doors, across the porch, and down the steps.

Gasping in the cold, misty morning air, I wait until the sick feeling passes. Then I begin walking again. When I come to a well, I drink deeply and scrub at the blood on my neck and cloak.

As the sun gleams through the haze, I go through a market, where men hawk wares from stalls with bright awnings. Past the market, I come to a wharf, maybe the same one from when we arrived here in Venice. It's busy with travelers and sailors and merchants, not at all like the wharf in Lynn, with its fishing boats. Still, the smell of pitch and wood and salt makes me think of home. I hoist myself onto a barrel out of the wind and let the sounds swirl around me: wooden ships creaking and groaning, waves slapping against the pilings, gulls screaming, the rumble of carts over wood.

Nearby, I can hear a man saying, "Roma," and then "Roma" again.

Rome, he must mean. Where my pilgrimage was supposed to take me.

I look up to see a priest talking to a sailor, who nods and gestures toward a ship. "Roma," the sailor says, nodding.

If I could find my way to the English hospice in Rome, I could wait there for Dame Margery. But how can I ever get there?

The priest calls to a group of nuns behind him, five of them, their habits as black and white as magpies. Two other women stand nearby—maidservants, I think, from their brown wool gowns. They all begin walking to the ship, the maidservants pulling a heavily laden donkey behind them.

I rise, watching them. All at once, I know what I must do. Without allowing myself to think about it, I straighten my cloak and follow them. Up the gangplank they go, the nuns giggling and chattering like a group of milkmaids, while the two servants haul at the donkey's bridle. My head lowered, my hand shielding my face, I stay close enough that I might be one of them. When the donkey digs in his hooves, I try to look as though I'm helping them with him. No one questions me.

Once over the gangplank, I move away from the nuns, mingling with the other people already on the boat, sailors and passengers. I find an out-of-the-way place at the side where I can look out at the horizon—and where no one will look at my face to see that I don't belong.

Someone taps my shoulder. A sailor. I'm caught.

The sailor says something, gesturing.

I take a step back, my eyes wide with fear. The sailor rushes into the place where I was standing and whips a rope around a metal spike. Then he yells to another sailor, who starts hauling on the other end of the rope.

I let out my breath in relief. I'm not caught, just in the way.

I find another place to stand and keep a careful watch any time someone approaches me.

Finally, we sail. Pulling my cloak around me against the cold wind, I watch as Venice recedes across the water. All I see are the red-tiled roofs, then only towers and church spires silhouetted behind me, and finally just a bumpy black line.

Venice is gone. I will never see Bartilmew again. I will never find out what happened to him.

I feel light-headed, hollow with hunger. My anger at Dame Margery bubbles up again and fills the hole in my belly.

When we reach our destination, I follow the nuns off the boat. I don't know where we are, but I hope it's the road to Rome. As they make their way through a town, I stay a little behind them. At the pace they walk, it's easy for me to keep up, and there are plenty of other people out, so I don't think they notice me.

The road is flat and leads us to another town. Oxcarts and men on horses pass by, and in the distance, I can hear bells before I can see the town gates. I hold back a little as the nuns enter, and then, when I realize the gates are clos-ing, I run, slipping through just in time.

The nuns don't go very far before they stop in the courtyard of a stone building. I watch from a corner as a servant bows and ushers them inside. Their maidservants take bags from the donkey's back, and a boy leads the donkey into a stable.

When the boy comes out again and everyone is gone from view, I cross the street and peer into the courtyard, then duck into the stable.

In the shadows, I can hear a horse nickering and another chewing, but I can't hear any people. I wait to be sure, then look for an empty stall. When I find one that's been mucked out recently, I settle in for the night.

My scrip digs into my side and I open it. Could I have left a cheese rind or a crust of bread inside? I dig through my fire-making supplies, my needle and thread, the blue bead I found in Cologne, the pebble my sister gave me, but I find nothing to eat. My fingers touch something metal, and I pull out Cook's cross, the one she gave me just before I left Lynn. It's green with corrosion. I rub at it, but it does no good, so I put it back and try not to think about how hungry I am.

Every few minutes, I jerk awake, sure the nuns have left without me. Every time, their donkey is still there, and besides, the night is still dark. When matins rings from a bell tower nearby, my shoulders finally relax enough to let me sleep the remaining hours until dawn.

A voice outside wakes me. Have they left? Fear grips me. Then I see their donkey in the stall next to me. I slip out of the stable and loiter in the streets, waiting for the nuns to leave.

From where I stand, I can see a square in the distance

with a well in it. I watch the courtyard, then decide to risk going for a drink. I have to, my head is so light with hunger, and my pig's bladder is long gone, left behind in Venice.

I get back just as the nuns are setting out. Soon, we leave the town behind and follow a path that heads into the hills. With fewer people traveling here, I have to stay farther behind to keep from being seen, but I never let them out of my sight.

At midday, when the nuns stop to rest and eat, I hide in a copse not far away and watch. They kneel and pray before their maidservants bring them bread and cheese and skins of water. My mouth waters and my stomach growls. I stop watching and try not to think about food, but I can't help myself. I see roasts turning on spits and the crackling the boy gave me long ago in Norwich. I smell Cook's pottage and Rose's curds and barley bread. Every meal I've ever eaten dances in front of me, just out of my reach.

When the nuns start up again, they walk even more slowly. I don't know how far Rome is, but at this rate, the Second Coming may happen before they get there. They walk until evensong, sharing the path with an occasional shepherd or farmer, and once, two well-dressed men who clop past on tall horses. I fall far behind. I'm so hungry I barely have the strength to keep up.

Night falls fast in the hills. As dusk settles around me, I slowly climb a rise and hear their voices. Then I see them, stopped right in the middle of the path, as if they plan to camp there for the night. The two servant girls are talking fast, arguing maybe. I watch.

It doesn't take me long to understand what they're

doing. Or *not* doing. They can't get a fire started. Now the priest is shouting at them, and one of the nuns shouts, too.

I touch the scrip at my waist, thinking of the flint and metal in it, the char-cloth I've been saving, all the little bits of flax and bark I've picked up on my journey, hoarding them like a jaybird.

I step forward. The priest sees me first. He narrows his eyes, flicking them behind me to see if I bring others with me, thieves perhaps.

The servant girls stand up and stare at me, and the nuns crowd behind each other, fear in their eyes. Fear of *me*.

I hold out my hands in a show of innocence. When the priest speaks, I shake my head to show I don't understand. "English," I say.

Then I come forward slowly, as if I were approaching a wounded dog. I kneel at the pile of twigs and sticks the servants have arranged on the path and open my scrip. No one says anything as I shape a little nest of kindling, just the way Bartilmew showed me. I concentrate hard, not wanting them to see my own fear as I strike my flint, fast as lightning, on the metal. A spark lights my char-cloth, and I drop it into the kindling nest, then hold the nest in my hands to blow into it. When the kindling catches, I place it in their pile of sticks and blow again, feeling the warmth on my eyelids as the flames spring to life.

Still kneeling, I look up at the faces around me: the priest, who stares from beneath furrowed brows; the servant girls, who watch me warily; and five nuns, their beatific smiles illumined by my fire.

One of the nuns, a solid woman who must be as old as Dame Margery, steps forward and raises me up. She says something and peers into my face. Her brows are a dark line under her wimple, and laugh lines crinkle the corners of her eyes. The lines deepen as she smiles at me.

I smile back.

As the two girls begin passing food around, the nun lowers herself to the ground and pats the grass beside her. I sit. When one of the maidservants gets to her, the nun speaks sharply. The maidservant frowns and gives her two portions, one for me.

Never have bread and cheese tasted so good.

The nun watches me as I eat and then gives me some of her own bread. I know I shouldn't take it, but I can't help it. It's all I can do to keep myself from snatching it from her; I'm so hungry.

When I've finished, she says something to me. I shrug to show I don't understand.

"Rome," I say, pointing at myself.

She shakes her head.

I try again. "Roma."

"Roma?" Her dark eyebrows lift.

I nod. Again, I point to myself, then walk my fingers over the grass and say, "Roma."

"Ah," she says as if she understands. A torrent of words pours forth, and the others look up, listening.

The priest speaks, sounding angry.

The nun puts her arms around me and answers him. Then two other nuns speak at the same time, looking first at the priest and then at my nun. Others join in, and one of them, a young nun with the longest, thinnest nose I have ever seen, moves toward me, her arm going around me, too.

The priest speaks again. This time he sounds defeated.

My nun smiles broadly and chatters away at me.

I smile and nod.

When the servant girls bring us blankets, my nun cuddles me close to her, just the way I used to do with Cicilly, the way Rose used to do with me.

Before I drop off to sleep, I look up to see the maid-servants crouching together by the fire, whispering to each other and scowling at me.

In the morning, my nun makes sure there's bread for me. I stay close to her as we walk, mindful of the maid-servants. One of them, who wears her hair in a single dark braid down her back, narrows her eyes at me when the nun isn't watching. Then she smirks at the other maidservant, a freckled, red-haired girl with a gap between her front teeth.

I look away. All I want is to get to Rome and find Dame Margery. It's the only way I'll ever get home.

By vespers, we come to a town with a hospice for pilgrims. There's warm pottage to eat and cots to sleep on, even for me. My nun, the thin nun with the long nose, and I all share a bed. Before we sleep, we kneel to pray, but my mind seems blank—I can't remember the words to prayers I've known all my life. I listen to the nuns' murmured litanies and try not to picture the knife raised high in the air over Bartilmew and Petrus Tappester. No matter how hard I screw my eyes shut, the image won't go away. I wish I knew what had happened. I wish I could pray for Bartilmew.

In the morning, when I try to help the nuns with their wimples and veils, they won't let me. Instead, they make the maidservants serve me, and when we start out again, they keep me between them as if I'm a pet lamb.

The rest of the trip passes the same way. I stay close to the nuns and keep my distance from the two maidservants, although I feel them watching me.

It's cold and we have mountains to climb, but compared to the Alps, these seem like mere hills. Most nights we spend in villages or hilltop towns, their castles and church towers looming over the landscape. The nuns moan and complain about the trip, and so do the maidservants. I may not be able to understand their language, but when they stop in the middle of the path to rub their feet or groan when they rise from the ground, I can see how hard this is for them.

One day, the young nun with the long nose takes off her shoe and reveals a bleeding blister. I tear a strip from my shift—it's up to my knees now, I've ripped so much off—and bandage her toe for her. You'd think she was Lazarus and I'd made her rise from the dead, the way she treats me after that.

As we prepare to get under way again, the maidservant with the dark braid walks past me and treads my foot hard, grinding it under her boot. Then her hand flies to her mouth and her eyes grow wide as she pretends it was all a mistake.

I look at her evenly, holding her eyes with mine to show her I understand what she's doing. What do I care for her? My anger is all for Dame Margery.

She smirks and skips back to her freckled friend.

I lose count of the days. We walk and walk, but when we come to monasteries or villages or towns, the nuns are always welcomed in and so am I. My nun tells people things about me that make them smile at me and offer me warm food and blankets to wrap myself in. I don't know what tale she tells, but I always smile back. And when the nuns hear Mass, I go with them, even though the incense chokes me and no prayers will fill the empty place inside of me.

Then one morning, the priest says something and points at a distant hill. I stare at it and realize it's not just a hill—it's a city.

The nuns all begin chattering at once. My nun clutches my hand. "Roma," she says.

My breath catches in my throat. Rome. Will Dame Margery already be here?

It takes till midday to reach the stone buildings we're heading for, a monastery, I think. There's a guesthouse outside the gates for the rest of us, but the priest disappears through the gates without a backward glance.

I'm looking around the guesthouse when my nun comes in, pushing a well-dressed woman in front of her. As my eyes take in the silk of the woman's gown and the fur at her collar, I drop a curtsy.

"English?" she says with an accent so strong I barely understand her.

"Yes, I'm English," I say, nodding.

My nun speaks to the woman in her fast, lilting language. The woman turns back to me and says haltingly, "Why you come here? Roma?"

Why have I come here? A flood of possible answers rushes to my tongue. I stop them all and say, "To find someone."

The well-dressed woman speaks to my nun. Then she turns back to me. "You go English hospice?"

I nod.

Again, the nun and the well-dressed woman confer before she turns back to me. She closes her eyes, and I can tell she's searching for words. "We take you English hospice," she says.

"Thank you," I say with another curtsy as she sweeps out of the room.

My nun shouts something, and the freckled maidservant peeks in the door. She frowns as the nun speaks to her, then leaves.

My nun pulls me into a hug, her cross digging into my chest. As she holds me away from her, she says, "Benedicite," a tear glinting in the corner of her eye. She smiles and turns me toward the door just as the two maid-servants both come in.

Suddenly, I understand. The servants will lead me to the English hospice. I square my jaw and glance at them.

Their smiles hold no hint of warmth. The black-haired one gestures with her head, and I follow, looking back at my nun, who sketches a cross in the air and holds up her hand in farewell.

We go through the courtyard and down a street, the two maidservants walking quickly and speaking quietly to each other. Every now and then, they glance back at me with furtive eyes.

We go through winding streets, and twice the black-haired girl stops to ask for directions, the second time out-side an inn where a woman is sweeping. I watch as the woman's mouth drops open. She covers it with her hand, looks at me, and lowers her eyes. Nervously, she points.

We start out again, entering a dark alley full of puddles and muck. I don't trust the maidservants, but I don't know what else to do except follow them.

The two of them whisper at each other furiously, as if they're arguing, but we keep going until we come to a sharp turn. I can hear loud voices from around the corner, and a horrible smell makes me wrinkle my nose. At first it seems sweet, but then it becomes the stink of rot and decay.

The black-haired maidservant turns to me. "Eenglish 'ospice." She points and I step forward. She pushes me so hard that I stumble and fall into a puddle of dark ooze. I look over my shoulder to see the two maidservants grab hands and run back the way we came.

When I hear a man's voice, I get up fast. I turn the corner and see two women with low-cut bodices standing in the alleyway, their skirts shorter than is seemly. A man holds one of them by the arm and slaps her face. She spits at him and he laughs at her.

Prostitutes.

I start backing up, my eyes wide. Just as I do, all three of them see me.

The man says something and beckons to me.

I stand frozen, staring at a scar that glows white on his cheek. He starts walking toward me.

The woman nearest me yells and grabs the man's arm.

I turn, slipping in the slimy puddle and hitting my knee, hard. Ignoring the pain, I scramble up again and run back down the alleyway, toward the light.

Breathing heavily, I listen for footsteps behind me. Nothing. Nor do I see the two servant girls, which is a good thing for them. I clench my teeth in anger.

The sun is getting low, and I have no food. I'll have to find the English hospice on my own.

Pain shoots through my knee when I start walking again. I limp down a street with stone buildings on either side. Two women carrying baskets pass me, and I call out, "English hospice?"

They look at me and recoil. One of them crosses herself and they both hurry away.

I look down. My gown and cloak are filthy, my skirt ripped to reveal my linen shift underneath—and my legs below that. I reach up and touch my hair. My braids have come loose, and a strand of hair sticks up on the side. Brushing at my clothes does nothing but spread the mud to more places. I pat my hair down, pull my cloak around me to hide my torn skirt and bare legs, and limp forward. The few people I pass avert their eyes when I get close to them.

A young friar comes down the street toward me, the

knots on his rope belt hitting his leg in time to his whistling, his blond curls bouncing with each step. I stop and watch him as he nears me, listening to the merry song he whistles.

The friar looks up as two sparrows wing past the roofline. He stops whistling to watch them, then takes up his song again as he walks.

I can't see his eyes, but his blond curls make him look almost angelic—or they would if his stomach weren't so round. Besides, he's a friar, and they help poor people, don't they? As he approaches, I put my hands together as if in prayer and say, "Benedicite."

The whistling stops and he looks at me, eyebrows lifted in surprise.

"English hospice?" I say, my voice cracking.

I know he is taking in my clothes, my hair. What must he think?

He furrows his brows, and I think I see compassion in his clear hazel eyes. He asks me something.

I shake my head and repeat, "English hospice," saying the words as clearly as I can.

"Ahh," he says as if he understands. He smiles and sweeps his hand out in a grand gesture for me to accompany him.

I breathe deeply in relief and follow behind him as he begins whistling again. I hope it isn't far. My knee hurts so much that it's hard to keep up. I grit my teeth and hurry along.

He picks up his pace to match a new, quicker melody. It's too fast for me. Two men pass, coming between me and my friar. "Wait!" I call, but he doesn't hear. "Please, wait!" I call again, my voice rising to a wail.

This time the whistling stops and he turns. As I limp toward him, he watches, frowning and shaking his head. When I get close enough, he points at my leg and says something, a lot of words that I can't understand.

I stare at him helplessly.

Still frowning, he glances up and down the street as if he's deciding something. Then he nods, says something else, and holds out his arm.

When I look at him, he gives me a kind smile before gesturing toward his arm.

This time I take it.

We go slowly, the friar supporting me. He chatters away as if we were old friends, occasionally smiling down at me or laughing. I'd smile back if I weren't too busy trying to walk. It's easier with his help, but every step makes me wince.

When we come to a corner, the friar releases my arm and motions for me to go first down a dark, narrow alley. We've only gone a short way when he touches my shoulder to stop me at a door. He opens it and leans his head in, as if listening. He calls out, but nobody answers. He stands there a moment, then speaks to me, gesturing for me to enter.

I step over the threshold and stop. It's pitch-black. If this is the hospice, where is everyone?

The friar puts his hand on my shoulder and says something in a quiet voice. He guides me farther in and to a wall. I feel a door, then stairs. He murmurs something and gently pushes me toward them. Climbing makes my knee hurt even worse, and I let out a whimper.

The friar shushes me, crooning like my sister used to when I came crying to her with some childish sorrow.

At the top of the stairs, he guides me through another door and to a place where I can sit. I lower myself onto a soft surface, trying not to groan. This can't be the hospice, but right now, I don't care. I just want to sit here and let the friar tend to me.

He says something, then goes out. I can hear him whistling as he descends the stairs and moves around down below. The whistling grows louder as he climbs up again. He appears in the doorway, his clean-shaven face lit by the oil lamp he carries. In the other hand, he has half a loaf of bread and under his arm, a waterskin. My stomach growls in anticipation.

The lantern flame flickers as the friar moves, and I look around the shadowy room. There's no bench, no table, nothing at all except the pallet I'm sitting on, a few tufts of straw sticking out of it, and a blanket folded neatly at its foot. Someone has swept the floor so clean that even Rose would approve, and I can smell lavender coming from the pallet.

The friar sets the lamp down near me, then puts down the bread and the waterskin beside it. As he sits on the floor, he says something and laughs, showing white teeth.

I watch him, but I don't understand the joke.

He pulls a piece off the bread and hands it to me. I take it and bite into the crusty loaf.

He speaks, his eyebrows going up in a question. When

I don't answer, he laughs again, then eats a piece himself. He tips the waterskin back and takes a swallow before he hands it to me.

The water feels cool on my throat. I give him the skin back and finish my bread.

The friar takes another long drink. He sets the skin down, smiles, and asks me another question.

When I shake my head to show I don't understand, he comes over to the pallet and sits beside me.

My mouth drops open, and my eyes widen with fear. I scuttle into the corner, as far away from him as I can get, my cloak clutched around me.

A look of hurt surprise crosses his face. Then his features soften. He holds his hands up, palms facing me, and rocks back so he's sitting on his knees on the floor, off the pallet. He speaks in a low, soothing tone, the way you would to a frightened sheep.

As fast as my fear came, it flees, shame taking its place. The friar has done nothing but help me. Tears prick at my eyes and I lower them.

When I look up again, he shakes his head, smiling his forgiveness. He points at me and pantomimes sleep, his face cradled on his hands. Then he points at himself and walks his fingers away. He's leaving.

I nod to show that I understand.

"Thank you," I say, and add a word I learned from the nuns. *"Grazie."*

He smiles again. Leaving me the lantern, he backs out of the room, taking the waterskin with him. I hear him going down the stairs, across a room, and out the door.

His whistling begins again, a slow, mournful tune this time. As it grows fainter, I feel my shoulders relax. This may not be the English hospice, but it's good enough for now. Slowly, sleep overtakes me.

A sound jerks me awake. I blink and look around me. The lantern has gone out, but enough gray light filters into the room that it must be morning.

Gingerly, I stand, testing my knee. It hurts, and beneath my skirt it's hot and swollen, but I think I can walk. I listen for voices downstairs, but the only sound I hear is mice scratching in the walls.

Where is the friar?

I lie back down to wait for him, but soon I'm standing again, too impatient to stay still.

Brushing at my cloak doesn't get any of the mud off, but at least I can comb my hair with my fingers and braid it neatly. I fold the blanket and leave it on the end of the pallet, then glance around the room. I wish there were some message I could leave for the friar, some way to thank him.

A noise downstairs makes me jump. I stop to listen, but now it's quiet again. Am I alone here? I don't know and suddenly, I shiver. What if I'm expected to pay for the room? I pull my cloak around me and step to the door.

The stairwell is dark and I creep downward, one step at a time. A loud creak stops me—the third stair. I stop, not breathing, and listen. Nothing. I take another step, then another, and finally, I'm at the bottom. It's too dark to tell whether anyone is there. Slowly, cautiously, I tiptoe across the room, feeling my way to the door.

As I let myself out, I see no one. Suddenly, a loud shout comes from down the alleyway. I startle like a rabbit and run.

After a few steps, I have to stop, my knee hurts so much, but when I look behind me, the street is empty— whoever it was wasn't shouting at me. Still, I don't like this place. Rickety wooden buildings loom over me, cutting out the early-morning sun, and I don't know my way.

I pull my head into my cloak like a turtle into its shell and skulk along the alley, keeping close to the walls, limping as quickly as I can. Not many people are out yet; it's that early. I dodge puddles and piles of dung, heading for the alley's end.

A man steps out of a doorway right into me. He says something, but I keep going, not even looking at him. My heart pounds so loudly in my ears that I can barely make out the noises ahead of me.

Finally, I emerge into a market, just behind a fishmonger's stall—I smell the tubs of eels before I see them. A woman with a kerchief over her head sees me behind the stall and shouts angrily, but I don't stop. I limp past women carrying baskets and a man pushing a wheelbarrow.

As I pass a stall with pots of something for sale, I hear a woman saying, "Look here, Constance, this is the kind to buy."

I duck around a man hefting a wooden tub. Suddenly, I stop.

English. That woman was speaking English.

I turn and see her, a small, thin woman sniffing at a pot and handing it to a tall girl beside her.

My heart beating wildly, I approach her. "Beg pardon," I say.

She squints at me, pushing the girl behind her.

"You speak English," I say.

"And what if I do?" She holds her basket in front of her protectively.

"I have to find the English hospice," I say. "I . . . I'm a pilgrim from England, from Bishop's Lynn."

She lowers her basket a little and looks me up and down. "A pilgrim, are you?" The girl comes out from behind the woman but stays a step back.

I nod. "I . . . I got lost."

The woman squints at me for a long time, not saying anything. Finally, she nods her head. "Well, you can come with us, then. I cook at the English hospice, and Constance works in the kitchen, too."

"You do?"

The woman nods.

I can't help myself. I burst into tears.

26

"There now, there now," the woman says, reaching out to give me an awkward pat. "Constance can take you to the hospice, and I'll finish up here."

I wipe my face with my cloak and stand shakily.

Constance peers at me from under lowered lashes, her shoulders scrunched up to her ears. She must not know what to make of me.

"God bless you," I say to the woman.

"God keep you. Now, get on with you both; I have things to do," she says.

We go through the crowded market, past stalls covered with canvas awnings. As we walk, I see pilgrims with staves and broad-brimmed hats pushing toward merchants selling trinkets and food. The smell of grilling mutton makes my mouth water.

"Are you a pilgrim, too?" I ask.

Constance shakes her head. "I live here, at the hospice," she says.

A group of black-robed monks passes us, followed by three monks wearing white. Just as they disappear through a stone doorway, people begin running and shouting, and I hear galloping hooves. Constance pushes me to the side of the street as a man on a tall horse races down the narrow lane, leaning low over his saddle, his red cloak billowing behind him. Dust rises and settles again as the clatter of hooves disappears. People step back into the lane, but I listen for more hooves before I move again.

"It's all right," Constance says, lightly touching my arm. "How did you get lost?" Her voice is so low I can barely hear it.

I limp along beside her, wondering how to answer. "My mistress left me in Venice. She'll be here, at the hospice."

Constance looks at me, her eyes wide. "She left you? That wasn't right."

I shake my head. "No, it wasn't." As I speak, I feel the truth of Constance's words. And I realize how easily Dame Margery could leave me again. I can't get home without her, but I might not ever get home *with* her, either.

"It wasn't the first time she left me," I say.

The way Constance looks at me, her eyes full of sympathy, prompts me to tell the whole story, my words tumbling out. I leave out the part about the fight between Bartilmew and Petrus, but all the same, I see the knife raised high in the air.

She shakes her head. "That was wrong of her." She gestures toward my leg. "Do you need to rest? It isn't far."

"I'm all right." And I am. Just knowing that we're near the hospice makes me feel like I could walk forever if I needed to.

She guides me down a lane, through a stone gate, and

into a dusty courtyard. "The women's dormitory is over there." She points. "And the men's, and there's the chapel and the refectory, where pilgrims eat. The dormitory on the other side is for the sick."

As I look, a white-haired friar hobbles from the chapel, his back bent almost double. He smiles and raises a hand. "Benedicite, Constance," he says. "And who have we here?" His words roll like a Welshman's.

"Benedicite, Father Morgan. This is a new pilgrim."

I duck my head and give him a little curtsy.

"And does this pilgrim have a name?"

"I'm Johanna, Father." It's been so long since I've heard my name that it sounds strange on my lips.

"Well, Johanna, welcome to the Hospice of St. Thomas of Canterbury," he says, taking one of my hands in both of his.

"Constance!" a child's voice calls.

Constance drops the friar a curtsy and runs toward a little boy leaning out of a door.

Father Morgan laughs. "Henry keeps his big sister busy," he says. "Now, my dear, there are beds through that door and water for washing." He lets his eyes linger on my filthy clothes and raises a bushy white eyebrow at me.

I blush. "Thank you, Father."

At the dormitory door, I peer in, blinking to see in the dim light. Rows of cots with blankets folded at their ends have packs and odds and ends scattered around them. On one cot, a woman sits braiding a girl's hair. On another, a woman sleeps, a round shape rising and falling under a blanket. I suck in my breath. Dame Margery?

Carefully, I pick my way between rows to get to her. I'm halfway there when the shape stirs, rolls over, and tosses the blanket back. It's not her.

Up and down each row I go, looking at the packs, trying to find the one I carried all the way from Lynn to Venice, the one with the pot that poked into my back, the one with my hood and my blanket.

A woman glares at me.

"I'm looking for someone," I say. "I thought I might recognize her pack."

She watches me suspiciously, as if I'm going to steal something. I'm hardly the one she should be worried about—Dame Margery is the pack stealer, not me.

I look at the packs by every single bed. None of them is Dame Margery's.

There's an empty cot in the corner, and I sit down heavily. Of course she's not here, I scold myself. She went to Assisi first. She'll be here; I know she will.

When I wake, afternoon sun streams through the open door. My knee feels better, but my stomach growls, and I think I must have missed the midday meal. I find the well and scrub at my face and hands, my cloak, my gown, leaving wet patches. Then I sit back on the cot and pull my needle and thread from my scrip. It takes the very last length of my thread to mend the tear in my gown, but when I'm finished, my legs are covered once again.

As I step outside the dormitory, Constance sees me and

comes hurrying across the courtyard. "Are you hungry?" she asks in her soft voice.

I nod at the same moment my stomach growls again.

Constance hides a smile behind her hand. She leads me to the kitchen, points me to a bench, and brings me a bowl of oatmeal. The smooth wood warms my hands, and I lift the bowl to my nose to savor the smell.

"Not good enough for you?" a voice says. I lift my eyes to see the cook from the market staring down at me. "You don't have to sniff at *my* meals," she says. "There's nothing rotten in there, to be sure."

"Beg pardon, mistress," I say. "It's not that, not at all. It just smells so good."

She harrumphs and stalks back to a table where she's chopping something.

I lift the spoon to my mouth and let the buttery oatmeal warm me. I have never tasted anything so good in my life.

When I'm done, I wash out the bowl and give it back to Constance, who ducks her head at me. "Did you find your mistress?" she asks.

I shake my head.

"You can stay in here, if you want to," Constance says. "As long as you keep out of the way." She points at the huge stone window, and I sit in the casement, looking around the kitchen. There's a two-ox fireplace against one wall, and Henry, Constance's little brother, works the bellows. Smoke puffs back at him, and I can see he's aiming the bellows at the wrong place, right into the ashes. I'd go help him if Constance hadn't told me to stay out of the way.

Beyond Henry, a big man with greasy hair and an apron tied around his waist handles a huge knife with ease, carving a hunk of meat into pieces, and a younger man, his head as round as a cabbage, throws down a huge bag of something. As the bag hits the floor, a cloud of dust rises up and the young man sneezes.

It feels strange not having anything to do. I reach into my scrip and pull out Cook's cross and turn it over in my fingers, looking at the green crust on it. I rub at it with my skirt, but it doesn't come off. I rub harder, but I can't get it clean.

When I look up, the cook is watching me. She comes over and squints at the cross. "You'll never get it clean that way." She goes away and comes back with a bowl of some kind of white paste and a rag. "Here," she says, pushing it at me. "You have to attend to it every day, or it'll end up like that again."

I rub and rub with the paste. When I wipe the cross off this time, only a few green spots remain. As a ray of the setting sun pierces a cloud and streams through the window, I hold up the cross. It gleams in the light.

i have a cot all to myself, and as darkness settles around the hospice, I pull the scratchy blanket up to my chin. Finally, after all these many days, I've found the place I've been searching for. But now that I'm here, I can't sleep. I wake, then doze, then wake again, sure I've heard my mistress's voice calling me.

The sound of bells wakens me in the morning, and I blink at the dark shapes of a dream I can't remember. Sleep-fuddled, I pull on my gown and follow the other women to the chapel for Mass. Clouds of incense burn my eyes and fill my nostrils, making me cough. It hurts to kneel, and the cold stone floor seeps into my bones. I can hardly wait for the Mass to be over.

When it finally is, the other pilgrims hurry off to shrines or markets. Not knowing what else to do, I go back to the women's dormitory and sit on my cot, examining the stitches in my newly mended gown. They're almost straight, and I didn't prick my fingers a single time. I wish I could show Cook.

On the far side of the dormitory, a door leads down a

narrow passageway. From the other end, I can hear familiar sounds: pots clanking, bread dough slapping on wood, a sharp voice saying, "That fire needs stirring."

I tiptoe down the passage, toward the smell of smoke and simmering oats.

When I peek through the door into the kitchen, the cook I met at the marketplace squints up at me from a chopping block. "You'll get your meal at midday, just like everyone else," she says when she recognizes me.

"Can I help?" I ask.

She gives me a long stare. "There's a new girl coming today, but she isn't here yet. You can stir those oats till she gets here."

I peer into the pot that hangs over the fire and see oats bubbling, making little *plop, plop* sounds as they boil. Their steamy scent smells like home.

"Are you going to let those oats burn?" the cook calls to me, and I pick up the wooden spoon to scrape the pot's sides and bottom.

As I stir, I look for Constance, but I don't see her. The big man I saw in the kitchen yesterday stands wiping his hands on his long apron, talking to someone just outside the doorway. He moves aside to let the young man with the round head come past him, his arms piled high with firewood. The young man drops the wood in the corner with a bright clinking sound and begins to stack it. Over at the fire, Henry is at the bellows, and just like yesterday, he's pointing them wrong, sending ashes into the air around him. He doesn't seem to mind, though—instead, he watches, smiling, as if he's having fun. When he gives the bellows an extra-hard pump and grins at the shower of ash he's created, I smile, too.

At that moment, Constance rushes through the door, her hair coming loose from her thin brown braids, a load of onions gathered into her apron. She stoops to whisper to Henry, who frowns and moves his bellows back to the glowing coals where they belong. Constance scurries on toward the cook who spoke to me and unloads her onions. As she does, the cook says something, gesturing with her head toward me.

Constance comes over and smiles a shy greeting. "I'll stir. Alice says will you help her?"

I hand her the spoon.

Alice looks around at me. "Still want something to do? Those pots over there need washing." She points at a stack of dirty kettles. "Water's in a barrel by the door."

I scrub the gruel that's stuck to the bottom of the kettles. Poor Alice must never be able to find someone who knows how to stir her pots. A fly buzzes around my face and I slap at it, getting water in my eye, but I keep scrubbing.

The kitchen is full of air and light, with huge windows facing the chapel. Brown-robed friars pass them, and every now and then, one comes into the kitchen to speak to the man wearing the apron.

Once, passing me, Constance whispers, "That's Master Alan, the head cook. Try to stay out of his way. But Wat's all right." She gestures at the younger man and smiles. As if he's heard his name, he looks over at us, his round face lighting up when he sees Constance. Then he squints his eyes shut and loses himself in a fit of sneezing.

Constance and Alice rush from task to task, and almost before I finish each job she gives me, Alice is ready with new orders. I chop carrots and onions, I stir pots and wash them, I measure millet and sweep floors.

When it's time for the midday meal, I'm still hard at work, but I don't mind. I think of Cook at home in Lynn and hear her throaty laugh. Alice isn't like Cook at all; she never laughs once all morning. But she never yells at me, either, even when I spill some porridge. Instead, she sighs and shakes her head before helping me clean it up.

After the rush of serving the midday meal dies down, Alice says gruffly, "You might as well eat in here with us."

Constance and Henry take their bowls to the hearth beside the big fireplace. Constance puts her hand on the hearth beside her and looks a question at me.

Gratefully, I join her. My knee throbs, and I burned my finger on a pot, and the onions made my eyes sting, but I feel wonderful.

"Don't know where that girl is," Alice says. "Hope she didn't find herself a position somewhere else, in some private house." She looks toward the door as if the girl will show up now that she's been mentioned.

Alice may want her, but I hope she's found another position, an easy one she'll never quit.

I stay in the kitchen all day, doing everything Alice asks and trying to do it quickly. Later, when darkness falls, I find my cot in the women's dormitory and fall into a dreamless sleep.

In the morning, after Mass, I'm back in the kitchen. I look around, but the new girl still isn't there. Alice sees me and doesn't say a word, just points to a kettle. I pick up the spoon and stir. Later, I help Constance weed the garden. She snaps weeds off at their stems, leaving the roots in the ground, so I show her how to work a stick into the dirt to get the weeds by their roots. "That way," I tell her, "they can't grow back as easily."

As we work, Constance asks me more about Dame Margery and my pilgrimage. "How could she do that to you?" She shows me a long, thin root she's pulled out intact. "If she comes here, will you go with her?"

I concentrate on a thick yellow root, digging the dirt around it with my stick, and don't answer.

"What would you do if she left you again?" Constance asks.

I look up to meet her steady gaze. I don't know how to answer.

"Johanna!" Alice calls from the kitchen.

The new girl must finally be here. My shoulders slump. Slowly, I rise and dust the dirt off my skirt. I don't want to go back to Dame Margery, but when she shows up, I'll have no choice. Pilgrims are only allowed to stay here for a few days before they have to give up their beds for new arrivals. When I leave, I'll have nowhere else to go—except with Dame Margery. There's no other way for me to get home.

I glance back at Constance just in time to see her snap a weed off by its stem. She gives me a guilty look. Then I step through the kitchen door.

"Hurry up, girl," Alice barks, slapping flour from her hands as I come in. "I thought you wanted something to do."

"I do," I tell her, not mentioning that weeding the garden *is* doing something.

"Come along," she says. She guides me through a doorway to a set of steps leading downward. "Let me show you how the wine works."

Suddenly, I feel light and happy. The new girl still isn't here.

I skip down the steps behind Alice into a cool, dim cellar and stand blinking until I can see again. Great wooden casks line the dirt wall, and a wooden counter stands in front of them.

"See this spigot?" Alice says, going behind the counter and picking up a cup. "You have to turn it slow, like this." She twists a knob on the first cask, and red wine dribbles into the cup. "You try."

The wine gushes out, spilling onto my hands, and Alice reaches up to shut the spigot off.

She shows me again and has me practice until I get it right. The cup the wine goes into is almost full. Alice takes it, looks at the stairs, and drinks it down. Then she gives me a funny look, the side of her mouth going up. I think it's a smile.

I grin back at her and give my head a little shake to show her I'll never tell anyone what she did. Well, maybe Constance.

She hands the cup back to me. "Three days of free wine for rich people, eight days for the poor," she says, patting at her mouth. "Think you can keep track?"

My eyes widen as I look at her. "I'll try my best." I have no idea how to keep track.

The side of her mouth goes up again—another smile. "Never you worry. Father Morgan has a system," she says. "You'll just need to stay down here from terce to nones turning the spigot. Any trouble, you call for Father Morgan."

I nod and we go back up the stairs.

"Alice," I say as we emerge into the light.

She stops in the doorway to look at me.

I take a deep breath. "If the new girl doesn't show up, the one you hired?"

"And what if she doesn't?" Alice says, frowning.

"Do you think I might have her job?"

She squints at me, her mouth drawn into a thin line. "That's something you'd have to ask Father Morgan." Suddenly, she turns her head, listening. "Hear that bell? That means a new group of pilgrims is here. Hurry, we have work to do."

28

as Alice and I get back to the kitchen, Constance comes running in, rubbing garden dirt from her hands. All of us scurry like chickens scattering from a cole-fox. Enough porridge, enough wine, enough beds for all the new pilgrims means the ones who have already been here for more than eight days have to leave. I've been here two. I try not to think about what I'll do if my days are up before Dame Margery arrives—or what I'll do when she comes.

Mostly, though, I'm too busy to think. We don't have time for a midday meal. Instead, we just grab oatcakes and munch them while we work. We keep going long into the evening, preparing things for the next morning. Even Constance's little brother Henry has to scrub pots so I can help Alice lift the heavy kettles.

I never get a chance to ask Father Morgan about a position in the kitchen, but I'm a little relieved about that. Asking Alice is one thing, but asking a priest? And what if he said no? Then what would I do?

By dark, I am too tired to worry about it, so weary that

I can scarcely make it to my bed. When I get there, I have to share it with two new pilgrims, a mother and her grown-up daughter. They're from York, and they want to tell me all about their journey and hear all about mine, but I mumble my apologies and crawl under the blanket. I know they must think I'm rude, but I don't have the strength to care. They kneel to say their prayers, and I shut my ears to their noise. I'm asleep before they finish their Paternoster.

The next day is as busy as the last—and then the bell rings again, two times. I look around to see Constance's mouth fall open and Alice shaking her head. "Hear that? New pilgrims yesterday, more today," she says, and lets out a sigh of exasperation. She looks at me. "Two bells? A big group of them."

I look at her in disbelief. A bigger group than yesterday?

Alice sees the expression on my face. "This is the slow season. Just wait till summer," she says.

By the next day, she no longer needs to tell me what to do. I glide from one task to the next, leaving for the wine casks when I hear the bells chime terce and running back up the stairs at nones to spoon bowl after bowl of oatmeal.

Finally, on the morning of the fifth day, things calm down so much that Alice sends Constance to the market—and tells me I can go along, too. It's cold and the sun has disappeared behind thick clouds, so we pull our cloaks around us and tuck our fingers inside to keep them warm. Constance leads me on what she says is the long route, past the river. We stand watching a stick bobbing on the brown water and then look up as a boat goes by, four men in tall red hats sitting importantly in it, red cloaks billowing behind them.

"Cardinals," Constance tells me before heading out again. We go through an alleyway, ducking to avoid wet linens that a woman is hanging out. "Those will never dry in this weather," Constance says.

As we emerge into a wider street, a dog with golden eyes and sharp ears barks at us, then joins us as we hurry toward the market, his tongue hanging out of his grinning mouth.

"We'll call him Fox, because he looks like one," I say.

Constance opens her eyes wide, then smiles and joins in my game. "We'll hide him from Alice—she'll never know he's there."

"Wat will help us find food for him."

"He can sleep with Henry and me—we'll be covered in dog hair, but he'll keep us warm."

"Wait, where did he go?" I ask, looking behind me.

Constance points and I see the dog nosing at a pile of something. "I guess that smells more interesting than we do." She gives me a rueful look.

"Goodbye, Fox," I call, but he doesn't look up.

"This way," Constance says, leading me around a corner.

The market opens before us, full of people and noise and delicious smells. Chickens squawk and men call out, hawking their wares, while a knot of pilgrims peers at the goods displayed under the canvas awnings.

I stand back watching while Constance stops in front of a stall, sniffing at little pots until she finds one that satisfies her. She hands a coin to the woman behind the wooden counter, who lets out a torrent of words, shaking her head and gesturing sharply, palm down.

I move up beside Constance, who whispers, "That's how much Alice told me it costs. That's all she gave me." Her face tells me how frightened she is.

"Here, give it to me," I say, taking the coin and the little pot from her. I sniff at it. It's some kind of spice, I don't know what, but it smells wonderful, tickling my nose and making me think of tales about knights journeying to far-off lands. Still, I wrinkle my nose in distaste and say loudly to Constance, "You would pay that much for *this*?" I don't think the woman behind the counter can understand my words, but I make sure she comprehends my tone. "Don't say anything," I hiss to Constance between clenched teeth. Then I speak loudly again, pointing at the pot. "This is terrible; it will never do." I shake my head dramatically and set the pot back on the shelf. "Come along."

The woman behind the counter says something, and I glance briefly over my shoulder at her, but I keep moving away.

Again she says something, and this time I look back at her, my eyebrows raised. She takes the little pot off the shelf and holds it up, her other hand outstretched, palm up.

With as much scorn as I can muster showing on my face, I return to the stall and take the pot from her. I sniff it again and shake my head.

The woman says something to me and I sigh, holding up the coin.

She snatches it from me and drops it into the bag at her waist.

"This will have to do," I say to Constance, and turn, holding my head as stiff and proud as a noble lady's.

We're outside the marketplace before we dissolve into laughter.

"How did you dare?" Constance says as I bow low and present her the pot of spice.

Grinning, I tuck my arm into hers, and we start back for the hospice. We haven't gone far before we come to a small church almost hidden between two buildings that tower over it. Constance stops, her face solemn again. "Let's go in," she says.

Reluctantly, I follow her. She kneels, crossing herself and lowering her head. I stand behind a column, waiting, swallowing the bile I feel rising in my throat. I think it's the smell of the incense that makes me feel so ill. I try to think of a prayer, but my mind feels blank. Cold from the stone floor seeps into my soles, chilling me. I wish Constance would hurry.

Finally, she's finished. She gives me a strange look as we go down the church steps, but she doesn't say anything until we're on the street. "My mother loved that chapel," she whispers.

"Your mother?" I drop my voice to a whisper, too.

She nods and tears glint in her eyes. She lowers them and then, after a moment, looks up at me, smiling. "Alice said you were going to ask Father Morgan if you could have a position at the hospice. What did he say?"

Now it's my turn to look away. "I haven't asked him

yet," I mumble. Every time I've seen him, I haven't been able to get up my courage, and besides, I've had too much to do. But with all the new pilgrims arriving, I have to do something fast, or I'll find myself out on the streets again, just like I was when I ran away from Petrus Tappester in Venice.

Neither of us speaks the rest of the way back to the hospice. The leaden skies seem to settle themselves around my heart.

Alice looks at us sharply when we come into the kitchen. We were away too long, and we both know it. But when she takes the jar of spice from Constance and sniffs it, her expression lightens. "This is very high quality," she says, sniffing again. "How did you get this much? How did you pay for it all?"

"You gave me the money," Constance says.

"You got all this for the coin I gave you?"

"No." Constance gestures toward me. "But Johanna did."

"Did she, now?" Alice gives me an appraising look, then takes the spice with her to her chopping board, closing her eyes and breathing in its scent again before she puts it away. She turns to see us watching her. "Those pots didn't clean themselves while you were gone," she says, but I can tell she's pleased.

I smile at Constance as we turn toward our tasks.

after Mass the next morning, I run back to the dormitory to drop off my cloak before I head to the kitchen. Just as I'm about to go through the kitchen door, I hear Alice's voice.

"She knows her way around a kitchen."

I stop to listen, my heart pounding. Has the new girl finally shown up?

"Did everything I asked, did it fast, and never complained."

When did all this happen? The new girl wasn't there when I went to bed last night, and it's too early for her to have been here today. Then I remember yesterday's trip to the market, and I kick myself for how long Constance and I took.

Someone else is speaking now. "She does have a mistress, doesn't she, though, who will be looking for her?" It's Father Morgan.

"A mistress?" Alice harrumphs. "Begging your pardon, Father, but what kind of mistress leaves a young girl alone like that in a foreign place?"

Realization dawns on me. It isn't the new girl they're talking about. It's me.

"Is that what her mistress says happened, then, Alice?" Father Morgan's voice is grave.

I hold my breath, listening.

"Haven't ever seen the woman, have I? But I believe the girl."

"So do I, Alice, so do I. But if she's bound to someone else . . ." His words trail off.

"Someone who's left her alone these past weeks," Alice adds.

"When the mistress shows up here, we'll see what she has to say."

Alice makes a sound of disapproval. "*If* she shows up."

Then I hear Father Morgan's footsteps coming toward me. What do I do—step into the kitchen and pretend I was just coming in, or go back to the dormitory?

"Johanna."

I'm caught. How did he know I was here? I come out from behind the doorway, my head down, my cheeks burning.

"Come, my child." He holds a hand toward me and I take it. "We need a new keeper of wine, and Alice needs a kitchen helper. She says you're a good worker. Will you take the job?"

My heart swells. Since I've gotten to Rome, no one has called me wicked or stupid or lazy the way Dame Margery did all the way from England to Venice.

I'm in a place where there's always food and warmth, and where I have no need to fear men like Petrus Tappester.

I nod. "Yes, please, Father."

"That's settled, then," Alice says. "You'll move your things in with Constance and Henry."

Father Morgan looks at me from under his bushy white brows and smiles. "And later, I'll show you my wine-measuring system."

I slide my eyes toward Alice, who gives me a sly look. I suppress a grin as I remember her cup of wine.

"Now, those pots." She points and turns back to her worktable.

"The pots will have to wait," Father Morgan says.

"Pots can never wait," Alice says. "If she's to help in the kitchen—"

"In the fullness of time, Alice, in the fullness of time. Come with me, child."

My breath catches in my throat. I don't know what's happening, and the last thing I want is Alice angry at me.

I glance over to see her mumbling something and bringing her cleaver down hard, splitting an onion in half.

"Don't worry about Alice," Father Morgan says, loud enough for her to hear. "She understands the relative importance of pots and souls."

Alice gives a sigh of exasperation, and Father Morgan smiles before he leads me out of the kitchen and across the courtyard.

Outside the chapel doors, he stops and turns to me, his face solemn. "You have had a hard journey."

I don't answer.

"On such a pilgrimage, there are many opportunities to sin," he says, and I stiffen. What has he heard about me?

Like he did before, Father Morgan reaches for my hand and covers it with both of his, warming mine. Under his white brows, his eyes are piercingly blue. He holds me in his gaze. "Many opportunities to sin, but few, I think, to confess."

I hang my head.

"Would you like for me to hear your confession, my child?"

I don't know what to say. I'm not ready for this, not at all.

Father Morgan puts a hand to my chin and lifts my head until I can't help but look at him again. "The Lord's forgiveness passes all understanding," he says, his voice low and calm.

A tear leaks out of the side of my right eye, and I brush at it angrily.

"Come along," he says.

I follow him into the chapel, dread in my heart. I haven't prayed in so long. How can I confess? I can barely enter a church without choking.

At the altar, he lowers his hood over his eyes. I kneel, careful about my knee. My mouth dry, I force out the familiar words, "Bless me, Father, for I have sinned." But I can't go on.

"Have you sinned in thought, my child?"

I nod, my eyes lowered, and feel sick.

"Tell me," he says, his voice gentle.

I open my mouth, but no words come out.

Father Morgan waits silently, but I still can't speak. "Have you felt envy toward another, my child?"

Have I? I don't think so. I shake my head.

"Anger?"

How did he know? I nod, and as I do, I say in a small voice, "I have been so angry, Father."

"Ahh." He nods. Little by little, he coaxes the words out of me, my rage at Dame Margery for leaving me, even if she is a holy woman, even if the Lord told her to. I tell him about what happened in Venice, how I deserted Bartilmew when he defended me against Petrus Tappester, how I don't know what happened to him.

It seems like I have talked forever, but when I stop, he says, "There's something else, isn't there, my child?"

There is, but I don't know how to say it.

He waits. And waits. I hear sparrows chittering in the rafters. Somewhere outside, a man calls to someone. Still, Father Morgan waits.

"The saints have forsaken me, Father." My whisper is so low, I'm not sure he hears me. If he does, what must he think of me? I cower, my chin lowered almost to my chest.

"Have they, now?" he says.

I keep my eyes down.

"You're sure you haven't forsaken *them*?"

I can't speak.

He doesn't say anything else about it, just gives me an easy penance, a Paternoster and an Ave at morning, midday, and evensong for five days. "Say the words," he tells me, "and the saints might just hear them." He crosses me, touching my forehead, my chest, my left shoulder and my right, then walks stiffly out of the chapel, leaving me before the altar.

I stay on my knees despite the ache. As Father Morgan's footsteps fade, I realize that nothing's changed. I still can't pray. And I didn't confess everything I should have.

Like about Hodge. The anger that's been knotted up in my belly for so long begins to loosen, but I clench my teeth, unwilling to let it go. I've been angry at my sister's husband for a long, long time, ever since I got to Dame Margery's. But it's not really Hodge; I know that now.

It's Rose I'm angry at. At Rose—and at myself.

All the hopes I've held on to about my sister and my father coming home again—they've all been dreams, nothing but dreams. I have been a fool.

Suddenly, without warning, the knot unties, emptying me of my anger and leaving me nothing but memories and the truth I've been hiding from myself.

Rose will never leave Hodge. She couldn't even if she wanted to, now that they're married. But she doesn't want to. I've seen the way she gazes at him, her eyes full of tenderness. She loves him. And with his three motherless children for her to take care of, how can she spare any love for me? Especially when I acted the way I did.

It was Rose, not Hodge, who made me go away. Hodge may have found me a place at Dame Margery's, but Rose told him to. I listened to them arguing when they thought I was asleep. I can scarcely think of it for the shame, yet the memory is too strong to ignore. Too much the truth.

"But she's your sister," Hodge said. "And she helps take care of the children."

"She acts like a child herself and makes more work for me," my sister said. "She needs to grow up. If she's not going to be any more help to me, she'll have to go into service and earn her own way."

Rose said that. About me.

I remember lying on my pallet in the loft of their cottage, feeling as if I had been slapped by her words. Had I really caused her more work?

Yes.

How many times did I sulk behind the cottage instead of milking the cow until her bawling brought Rose running to do it herself? How often did I wander off into the fields looking for daisies and butterflies instead of watching the sheep? I didn't help Rose with the little boys as I should have—I let them run crying to her when her arms were already full of washing or baking or brewing. I refused to smile at Hodge, even the time he brought me a robin's nest with three bright blue eggs in it. Or when he told Rose he was the one who had spilled the oats when he had seen me do it.

But I've bottled up Rose's words and refused to think of them so I could blame Hodge instead. I thought he would help my father with his debts, but I was wrong. My father's debts were too much for ten farmers to pay, let alone just Hodge. Even so, Hodge would have paid them if he could have.

Still, it seems as though nothing bad happened until Hodge began stopping by our cottage to see Rose.

A tear plops onto my cloak.

I'll never live with Rose and my father again. I know that now.

And I know it's not Hodge's fault.

Another tear trickles down my cheek, leaving its salt taste in my mouth. Then another, and then another.

When the tears finally stop, I breathe in shakily.

A calm emptiness fills me.

"Ave Maria, gratia plena," I whisper. "Hail Mary, full of grace." This time the rest of the prayer comes to me and I say it aloud. Then I say my Paternoster.

When I look up, a shaft of light illuminates a stained-glass window. St. Michael looks down on me, his scales in his hand, weighing a tiny, naked soul.

the pots are still waiting when I get back. I stopped at the well to wash my face before I went in, but it didn't help. One glance would tell anyone I've been crying.

As I go to my scrubbing, Wat gives a mighty sneeze.

I look up at the sound, and Constance catches my eye, giving me a nod of understanding. I try to smile at her, but when my lower lip quivers, I turn quickly to my work.

I'm glad of the tasks Alice sets me, especially when I can lean over a boiling pot and feel the steam bathing my eyes. Or when she sends me to the cool, dark cellar to measure wine. "Taste it first to make sure it hasn't gone bad," she says, making a funny face as if she's in pain. I'm on my way down the stairs before I realize she was winking. I smile and feel my face begin to relax.

By the time the sun is high enough to reach over the chapel roof and into the kitchen window, just when I'm ready to sit and rest my aching knee, a bell rings, twice. Another big group of pilgrims, but this time I don't even blink; I just measure more oats into the kettle. After the fourth handful of oats, I suddenly stop, remembering what this means. Other pilgrims will have to make way for the new ones. But not me. I have a place now and a bed with Constance and Henry.

There's no time for me to run to the chapel for the midday prayers Father Morgan assigned me as penance, so I say them while I'm stirring the kettle. As I do, I remember Rose teaching me the words, our voices blending as we said them together, kneeling beside the pallet we shared.

In the afternoon, Father Morgan shows me his system for keeping track of how much wine each pilgrim gets. I know I'll never be able to remember it, but when he asks me, I tell him I will.

He smiles. "It's like praying, child. Keep practicing and it will get easier."

I hope pouring gets easier. Jars and flasks are easy, but wineskins and pigs' bladders collapse every time I try to fill them, spilling wine onto the counter and the dirt floor below.

When our work is finally done for the day, Constance shows me the little alcove hidden behind a curtain where she and Henry sleep. The cot is against the wall, and on the other side is the kitchen chimney. Delicious heat seeps from it, warming the blanket.

Henry is already asleep when Constance and I kneel together beside the cot to pray. I can feel her looking a question at me, but I lower my head and begin my Paternoster. She joins in, and then we say our Ave.

As we climb into bed, Henry wakes up enough to give me a hug. Then, startled, he opens his eyes and murmurs,

"Thought you were Constance," before he's sound asleep again. Constance and I smile at each other before she pushes Henry over to make room for all three of us.

The next day, I'm standing behind my wine counter, struggling with a little old woman's pig's bladder. She bobs her thanks over and over, her metal pilgrim's badges clinking with every nod as I hand the bladder back to her, its outsides as wet as its insides from where I misjudged the spigot. There's more wine seeping into the dirt floor than there is in her pig's bladder. At the rate I'm spilling it, all the pilgrims, rich and poor, will have to make do with three days' worth of wine. Maybe two.

"Sorry, mistress," I say.

"Never you mind, dearie, never you mind. You're doing God's work." She bobs her way out of the cellar, clinking up the stairs, and I look up to see who's next. Someone in a dirty white skirt.

My eyes widen and my breath catches in my throat.

"So *here* you are, you wicked girl." Dame Margery steps up to the wine counter.

I stare, unable to move. Her veil is as badly pinned as ever, and a dark stain marks the front of her white gown, as if she'd dribbled wine down it.

"Well, I see the Lord took care of you." She looks me over.

My legs remember to curtsy and I dip my body to her.

"Since you're here, you can get me my wine." The flask

she sets on the counter will hold twice as much as I'm supposed to measure out for any one person. "You can't imagine how hard this trip has been for me, but the Lord watched over me." She crosses herself. "Well, go on, then," she says, pointing at her flask.

Concentrating carefully, I fill it to the brim without spilling a single drop.

"Easy with that," she says as I hand it to her. "Now, come along." She turns toward the stairs.

I grip the edge of the counter. "No, Dame Margery." My voice is a feathery whisper, so small I can barely hear it.

She turns back to me, hard lines between her eyebrows. "I said, come along, you disobedient girl. Have you lost your hearing? There's work to be done."

I close my eyes and bite the inside of my lip. Louder this time, I say, "No, Dame Margery."

I open my eyes to see hers narrow. "No? What do you mean, *no*? You do what I tell you."

I train my eyes on her upper lip, avoiding her gaze. My fingers press the rough edge of the countertop so hard I can feel the wood biting into my bones. "My place is here now," I say.

Her eyes narrow again, and this time I look directly into them.

She sets down her flask and points at me. "Of all the ungrateful servants, you are the worst. The Lord will punish you for this." As she steps toward the counter, I back into the cask behind me.

"You," she says, gesturing. Her hand sweeps the flask

off the counter. It crashes to the floor, sending pot shards and wine everywhere. "Now look what you've done, you wretched girl."

A stair creaks and I see a brown robe coming down to the cellar. Father Morgan. He stops at the bottom of the stairs and looks from Dame Margery to me and back again. Then he looks at the broken flask on the floor and nods.

"Is it Margery Kempe?" he says, and my mistress turns to him. "I've heard much of you."

"This girl—" she says, her voice harsh.

"Never mind the spill; she'll clean it up. She's a good girl," Father Morgan says. "Come, you must tell me how the Lord speaks to you. Is it true that his voice sounds like sweet music?"

Dame Margery's voice softens and she smiles. "Yes, Father, and sometimes it's like a little bird, a redbreast, singing merrily in my right ear."

Father Morgan escorts her up the stairs, Dame Margery talking all the way.

I gulp in one breath and then another and look at the creases in my fingers, where I've pressed them into the counter's edge. My knees are trembling so hard that I have to lower myself to the floor, where I sit amidst the pieces of my mistress's broken flask.

My mistress? No, I can't be her maidservant anymore. People here treat me like I matter, like I'm worth something. To Dame Margery, I'll never be more than chaff, something she can kick out of her way when she's tired of it.

Besides, Constance is right. If I were to go with her, how long would it be before she abandoned me again?

But without her, how will I ever get home?

My tears start slowly, but then they come thick and fast, faster than my mistress ever cried on the way to Venice.

What will become of me?

I stare at the patterns in the wood of the wine cask. They run along together like currents in a river. Then my eyes fill again. I don't know if I'll ever see Rose or my father again.

A sob escapes my throat. I gulp in air, but I can't seem to breathe.

Just then, I hear a noise, feet coming down the steps. A pilgrim, needing wine. I wipe furiously at the tears with my sleeve, but it doesn't stop them.

When I stand, I see it's not a pilgrim. It's Constance. She catches my eye, then steps around the counter and pulls me into a hug. My tears start all over again.

When I can finally breathe, Constance rubs my back the way my sister used to. Together, we clean up the broken pieces of Dame Margery's flask.

"Your porridge is ready," she whispers. "Alice sent me to find you."

I nod and wipe my face on my apron.

As she leads me to the kitchen, Constance says, "I like the way you braid your hair. Will you help me do mine that way?"

I nod again. I can't speak, but my heart is full.

31

I keep as far out of Dame Margery's way as I can, but it's not easy. To reach the alcove Constance and Henry and I share, I have to go through the women's dormitory. When we are finished in the kitchen for the day, I stand at the dormitory door, listening for Dame Margery's voice, but I don't hear it above the low murmurs of women and the sound of a child crying.

In the flickering candlelight, pilgrims make dark lumps on the cots, and it's hard to tell who is who. My toe stubs against somebody's pack. Mine. I glance at the cot, but Dame Margery isn't here yet. The pack is the one I carried all the way from England to Venice, the cooking pot poking me in the back the whole way. The one with my hood in it. I stretch my hand toward it. A noise makes me snatch my hand away as if I've been burned.

I scurry into the alcove and duck behind the curtain, my heart pounding. Slowly, I get my breath back and climb into bed. I pull the blanket all the way over my head, hiding until Constance and Henry come crawling into bed with me.

Even after they're both asleep, I lie rigidly, listening for Dame Margery's voice. Finally, my eyes fall closed.

She's asleep when I get up the next morning, sharing a bed with a gentlewoman, both of them snoring lightly. I tiptoe past them and go down the passageway into the kitchen.

Only Alan, the head cook, is there, yawning so hugely his eyes are closed and he doesn't see me. I blow the fire awake and set out the stacks of porridge bowls.

Alice comes in from the courtyard, one pin in her mouth, one in her hands as she arranges her wimple. She gives me a quick nod, and I go to the sack of oats. One, two, three, four, five, six handfuls go into the kettle of water. I give it a stir before I haul it to the fire.

By the time Constance and Henry have come into the kitchen, I'm sitting in one of the huge window casements, blowing on my bowl of porridge to cool it and watching a sparrow hop along the eaves of the dormitory roof, cocking its head this way and that.

Constance peers past me to see what I'm watching. "Like in Father Morgan's sermon," she says.

I look at her, confused.

"Remember? He said the poor man was like a sparrow, alone on the housetop. Henry, watch out!"

The bellows fall over with a clatter. Henry looks up sheepishly.

"Be careful!" Constance says. "Are you all right?"

He nods and she goes to him, folding him in her arms.

I finish my porridge and turn to last night's pots. Then I measure millet for today's meals and chop the pile of onions Constance brings in until it's time for me to attend to the wine.

Down in the cellar, a long line of pilgrims waits for me, but I only spill wine once, when a pig's bladder springs a leak. I don't see Dame Margery at all.

When the line dwindles to nothing, I wipe the spigot and the counter the way Alice showed me and start back up the steps.

A shadow blocks the light. I stop midstep.

Dame Margery towers at the top, glaring down at me. She doesn't say anything, just stares at me, a line creasing her brow.

I take a deep breath and start back up the stairs. When I reach the top step, she doesn't move.

"Beg pardon, Dame Margery," I say, squeezing around her in the narrow passageway.

She doesn't speak, but I can feel her eyes on my back as I walk away.

"Johanna!" Alice's voice.

I let out the breath I didn't know I was holding.

"Come tell me how to cook this rabbit," Alice calls.

Rabbit? If she only knew. I smile and skip toward the kitchen. The rough stones feel comfortable, and I know just where to lift my feet to keep from stubbing my toes on the wood of the threshold.

Once I'm there, I see the rabbit will have to wait. Father Morgan stands by the courtyard door, motioning me over.

My heart catches in my throat. What if he says I have to go with Dame Margery?

"How long have you been in Dame Margery Kempe's service?" he asks me as I get near him. The kitchen grows quiet. Alice stands with her arms folded over her chest, watching us. Constance shushes Henry's humming. Wat stifles a sneeze, and even Alan, the head cook, stops carving a side of meat and looks up.

I try to remember. "I was hired at the Michaelmas Fair," I say, thinking back.

"Hmmm." Father Morgan shakes his head and I cringe. Then he looks back at me. "This harvest just past?"

I shake my head. "No, Father, the one before that. We left on our pilgrimage just before the fair."

"Ahh, I see," he says, and suddenly, I see, too. Servants are hired for the year at the Michaelmas Fair, and wages for the next year are paid. We left before the fair, so Dame Margery couldn't have paid Hodge and my sister. They must be furious. I've been working since October without any pay at all.

I smile at Father Morgan. "Then may I have the position?"

He nods. "You have it already. As far as I can figure, you started when you got here."

I take a deep, happy breath. "Thank you, Father."

He smiles and glances over at Alice, who gives him one of her funny grimaces. When he goes out the door, sound returns to the kitchen as everyone goes back to their tasks. Wat gives me a shy pat on the shoulder as he passes me, and Constance doesn't stop smiling all afternoon. Alice might be smiling, too, but it's always hard to tell.

That evening, the stream of pilgrims lightens, and

things are so calm that Alice serves out six bowls of por-ridge, one for herself, one for Alan, one for Wat, one for Constance, and another for Henry. And a bowl for me. She pulls the bench up to the long wooden table where we do our chopping and calls us all over.

When I get to the table, Alice hands me two dirty sliv-ers of metal. One is round and one is half-moon shaped. I look at them and back at her.

"It's your first pay," she says.

I stare at the coins, the dark grime etched into their edges. They feel cool and heavy on my palm. I don't even know what they're worth—they must be Roman. I squeeze my fingers around them, then open my hand and listen to the clink as I toss them.

When I look up, everyone in the kitchen is watching me. Wat bursts out laughing, and Constance hides her grin with her hand. Henry giggles. I look at Alice and see the side of her mouth pulled up into one of her peculiar grins.

Then we sit down to eat, just like we're a family.

For two more days, Dame Margery makes her home in the hospice, glaring at me whenever I pass her but never speaking to me. I hear her weeping in the chapel and telling other pilgrims about her visions, but she pins up her wimple and veil by herself. The veil hangs lopsided, and greasy fingerprints mark the edges of the wimple.

On the third day, when I tiptoe past her bed at dawn, she isn't there. Neither is the pack with my hood in it.

"Didn't you hear?" Constance says when I ask her

about it. "A rich woman invited her to stay in her house. Didn't you see the servants coming to get her last night?"

I shake my head slowly.

"Their clothes must have been made of silk, and they were just servants!" she says.

I open my mouth, then close it. Dame Margery is gone? A ball of fear forms in my stomach. How will I ever get back to England?

As I pour wine for today's pilgrims, I can't stop my fear from growing. I look at each pilgrim, their faces, their clothes, and wonder if I could travel with any of them. It's a long, dangerous trip. Who could I trust? How would I ever pay my way? The coins Alice gave me won't get me far, that I know for sure.

After the last of the pilgrims disappears up the steps, I lean back against the wine casks, inhaling their scent of oak and summer sun, and wonder what's to become of me. I wonder where Bartilmew is by now. In the Holy Land, I hope, a place even stranger than Rome. I think of him plodding along behind his mistress and her husband, carrying her heavy pack without complaint. I hope he's safe.

Alice's voice startles me from my thoughts. "Johanna? Where are you?"

I trudge back up the steps, making my way to the kitchen.

As I come in, Alice gives me a sharp look. "Hurry up. There's work to be done." She gestures toward a stack of wooden bowls.

Constance raises her eyebrows to ask if I'm all right, but she doesn't say anything. She starts handing me bowls to dip porridge into to take to the sick people the friars take care of. I fill bowl after bowl, trying not to think about Dame Margery.

"Careful!" Constance says, and I realize a dipper full of porridge has landed on the floor.

"Beg pardon." I turn my attention back to the bowls.

Alice comes over and I stiffen.

"Father Morgan is away till nightfall, and some of the brothers, too. I'll need you to help feed the sick, Johanna."

I nod, relieved. That's the second time I've spilled porridge—the second time that Alice has seen, anyway—but she's never yelled at me.

"When you finish with those, take that tray to the dormitory and help the brothers serve them." She marches back to her worktable.

The tray is huge and heavy. Constance helps me navigate it through the kitchen. I cross the bright courtyard, staggering under the weight of all that porridge, looking for a place to set it down for a moment. There isn't one. I keep going. At the dormitory for the sick, I have to kick the door open, and the tray sways dangerously.

A friar rushes to help, taking the tray from my hands and setting it down.

I watch the two friars in their brown robes move from bed to bed, delivering the bowls. Old people with slack, spotted skin lie feebly on some beds. In another, I see a little boy with twisted legs, his mother sitting beside him. Near them is a man with a cloth tied around his eyes. The brothers whisper words of comfort and encouragement to them all. One friar leans over to spoon porridge into the mouth of a woman who can't move her arms. The other friar comes back to get more bowls. "You start in the next room," he says, pointing me toward a door.

I stack five bowls on top of each other, the way the friar has done, praying that I won't drop them, and walk carefully to the other room. Just through the door, there's a place to set them down. As I do, the stack wobbles. As the top bowl falls, I reach out and catch it. Good thing Alice wasn't here to see that.

Behind me, I hear a voice. "The little serving maid? Johanna?"

I stop. I can't move, lest it be a dream.

"Is it you, Johanna?"

Slowly, I turn.

In the cot behind me, John Mouse leans back on his elbows, watching me.

John Mouse, here in Rome? I can't believe it! I want to weep and laugh and dance all at once.

He holds out his arms and I can't stop myself. I go to him, there on his cot, and let him wrap his arms around me, even if it isn't seemly.

When I hear a man clearing his throat, I jump away. The friar. He casts an odd glance at me, then says something in another language. John Mouse answers him, so it must be Latin.

"I want to know everything," he says to me, "but this good brother says he needs you now."

I nod, blinking back tears.

"Good," he says, and lays his head carefully on his pillow.

I follow the friar. Together we feed a man who can't sit up, the friar cradling him in his arms while I spoon porridge into his mouth and wait for him to swallow. Some of it dribbles down his chin and the friar wipes it off, like a mother feeding a baby.

With every spoonful, I want to look at John Mouse. His

face was so pale and drawn, but he had the same brown eyes I remember from so long ago, before he fell in the Alps.

We go from bed to bed, sometimes handing out bowls, sometimes feeding people. As I sit on an old woman's bed waiting for her to take another bite, my foot jiggles with impatience. She looks down at my leg and says meekly, "I'm so sorry, child. I can't go any faster."

Chastened, I still my foot and smile encouragingly as I feed her another spoonful.

Finally, I've served the last bowl. I look at the friar.

"Go to your friend," he says.

I skip around beds, passing the other friar, who narrows his eyes at me in disapproval. Let him frown. What do I care?

But when I get back to the room John Mouse is in, I'm suddenly shy. My hand goes to my hair, and I smooth my gown, wishing it wasn't so dirty. Then I peek around the doorway.

John Mouse lies on the bed, his eyes closed. His face is even thinner than I realized, his skin pale as an angel's. His lashes flutter open. He looks at me and grins.

My heart beating fast, I perch at the end of his cot while he pulls himself up into a sitting position.

"Ah, my little serving maid," he says. "I hoped I might find you here."

"You did?" My words come out in a squeak.

"This is Rome, isn't it?" His eyes dance, as bright and merry as I remember. "Where's your mistress?"

I look down. "She's not my mistress anymore."

He raises his eyebrows.

"She left Venice without me," I say. When he encourages me with his eyes, I tell him how I got to Rome.

"You just followed the nuns onto the ship? And no one stopped you?" He laughs. "That took some courage. Then what happened?"

I tell him how I walked behind the nuns until I built the fire for them and they took me in, and how Father Morgan hired me to work in the kitchen. There's a lot I don't tell him. It hardly seems to matter now how cold and hungry I was, or how alone and afraid I felt. I don't say anything about the fight between Bartilmew and Petrus Tappester, either, and nothing about how even prayer deserted me.

He gives me a long, solemn look. "Your way hasn't been easy, has it?" he says.

I drop my eyes. Then I look back at him. "Where's Thomas?"

"In Bologna, at the university. He'll be a brilliant lawyer."

"You're going to study law, too, aren't you?" I ask.

"I *was* going to. Now I don't know." He makes a wry face, as if it doesn't matter.

"I'm sorry, John Mouse," I say.

"Beware of dreams."

"They mock us with their flitting shadows."

His eyes widen in surprise. "Where did you learn that?"

"Have you lost your memory?"

"Did I teach that to you?" he asks.

I nod, and he shakes his head, smiling. Then he closes his eyes and covers them with his long, pale fingers.

"John Mouse?" I say in a worried voice.

He keeps his eyes closed long enough for me to say a

silent Ave. That long. Finally, he opens them again. "The relics in Rome have healed people much worse off than me," he says, "but the journey here was difficult." He takes an unsteady breath and looks right into my eyes. "The relics will only help if I can get to them, and I don't think I can do that alone. Will you help me get to St. Peter's?"

As he speaks, the bells toll vespers, and I realize how late it is. "I have to go," I say, looking around as if I'll see Alice standing behind me, frowning. "But I'll find out about St. Peter's."

He reaches for my hand. His fingers feel soft and warm against my work-roughened palms. I pull back, but he doesn't let go. "You won't desert me, little serving maid."

I shake my head.

At the door, I look back. His eyes are already closed.

Father Morgan gives me permission to take the morning off from my wine duties. He also gives me directions to St. Peter's.

And so it is that I see the altar of St. Veronica in St. Peter's great church. On feast days, when St. Veronica's handkerchief is displayed, you can see Christ's face imprinted on it. If you traveled from overseas and prayed to it on a feast day, John Mouse says you would receive twelve thousand years off your time in Purgatory. Today, a curtain hides it, but we kneel and pray before it, anyway. He thinks the saint might help his head.

I help him up and steady him. He closes his eyes, then says, "Have you ever prayed to St. Pega, Johanna?"

I nod. How did he know? "That's St. Guthlac's sister. She's from the Fens, near where I grew up."

"Then come with me." He leads me around a column and through the crowds to the other side of the great nave. We walk slowly, John Mouse leaning on my shoulder, and pass altar after altar. A white-robed monk sits in front of one, holding a pen and a sheet of parchment.

"What's that monk doing?" I ask.

"If any miracles happen, he'll write them down so everyone will know."

A miracle? I look back, hoping to see a blind man regain his sight or a withered leg become whole again, but the crowd swallows up the altar and I can't see anything.

John Mouse stops to lean against a column and puts his hand to his forehead. When he's ready again, we push into the crowd.

"Here," he says, pointing at the stone floor. "St. Pega's tomb."

How did a saint from the Fens end up here, so far from home? Perhaps the same way I did.

At my belt, I wear my scrip. I reach into it and pull out the two coins Alice gave me. I had thought to save them to help buy my passage home. Now I have a better idea. "How many candles do you think this will buy?" I hold the coins out to John Mouse.

His eyes widen a little. "Where did you get that?"

"I work at the hospice, you know. It's my first pay."

"Are you sure you want to spend it all?"

I nod.

John Mouse stops a deacon and asks him something in

Latin. He turns back to me. "You could light all of the candles they've got here at St. Pega's tomb with that."

"Will you wait for me?"

He holds my eyes in his for a moment, then smiles and sits at the base of a column.

I put the money in the little metal box beside the tomb. Then I start lighting candles. First I light one for John Mouse, since he's right here for St. Pega to see. I ask her to help his head and his eyes. Can he still read books? How can he be a scholar without them?

Then I light candles for Rose, for my father, for my mother, and for the baby who died when my mother did. I light one for Hodge—it will have to do for his three little boys, too, because I can't even remember all their names.

As I light a candle for Cook, I pull her cross out of my scrip. It gleams in the flickering flames, and I touch it to St. Pega's tomb. Then I tuck it back into the scrip for safekeeping until I can take it back to her. The next candle is for Cicilly, who I haven't thought about for so long I'm ashamed of myself.

Bartilmew comes after Cicilly. I rifle through my scrip until I find the blue glass bead I picked up outside the cathedral in Cologne. Carefully, I set it in a carved indentation in the tombstone. The blue might help St. Pega recognize Bartilmew—it's the color of his eyes.

The nun who took me in on my trip from Venice to Rome gets her own candle. So does the friar who helped me my first night in Rome. Alice and Constance and Henry and Father Morgan do, too. I think for a minute and add

Alan and Wat to the list. "If there's anything you can do about Wat's sneezing, please help him," I ask the saint.

Finally, there's only one candle left. Who should I light it for? I think about my journey from Lynn, over the English Sea, through fields and forests and mountains, to Cologne and Constance, to Bolzano and the monastery in the Alps, from Venice to Rome. With a shudder, I remember the mercenaries, but the memory of warmth and the smell of baking bread chases them away when I remember the black-haired servant girl who let me sleep in the oven high in the mountains.

I'll make it back to England someday. I'll find Rose and Hodge and my father again. I know I will.

As people walk past, disturbing the air, I watch my flames flicker, leaping like dancers on Midsummer's Eve. Finally, I light the last candle and kneel.

"Please," I pray to St. Pega. "Take care of Dame Margery. Keep her safe."

When I stand and turn, John Mouse is watching me, candle flames reflected in his dark eyes. I reach out my hand and help him to his feet.

He steadies himself, leaning against my shoulder.

"Are you ready?" I ask.

He nods.

I guide him into the stream of people making their way through St. Peter's great church.

"Come," I say. "Let's go home."

author's note

We may not know when or where Johanna was born, or even her real name, but she really existed. So did her mistress. *The Book of Margery Kempe* is the first autobiography written in English, and in it, Margery tells the story of her pilgrimage to Rome. Reading it, I was struck by the remarks Margery made about her maidservant, who she said was disobedient, someone who wouldn't do as she was told and who wouldn't take her mistress's advice.

According to Margery, before they even left on their pilgrimage, a holy man warned her that her maidservant would give her trouble and would turn against her—as she believed happened in Rome. During the pilgrimage, when the company arrived in Constance, the rest of the pilgrims wouldn't let the maidservant accompany Margery. Whom did Margery blame? The maidservant, of course. And in Venice, as Margery told it, the maidservant cooked meals for the entire company and washed their clothes instead of attending to her mistress alone—as if that were fun! When Margery arrived in Rome, she said she found her maidservant at the Hospital of Saint Thomas, "living in great wealth and prosperity, for she was the keeper of their wine." When I got to that line, I cheered for the maidservant and wondered how she had accomplished such a feat. I wanted to know how the story would sound if the maidservant was the one who told it. Thus, Johanna—and her book—came into being.

Ironically, for all the literary credit she gets, Margery Kempe was illiterate—as Johanna would have been. She dictated her memoirs to a priest several years after her pilgrimage. Because Margery saw her book as a religious autobiography, she focused on her relationship with God and his saints instead of on the sorts of details we might want to know today. She said nothing about how cold it was crossing the Alps in late autumn or what a wool cloak felt like in the rain or what she heard and smelled and saw in the markets of Venice. I had to rely on other pilgrims' accounts to fill in many of the details. Margery did tell about the arguments she had with her fellow pilgrims, several of which resulted in her being kicked out of their company. Once, one of the other pilgrims was so angry at Margery that he said he wished she were out to sea in a bottomless boat. Another time, her fellow pilgrims ripped the bottom part of her gown away, perhaps to make her look foolish. Often, her fellow travelers worried about her preaching. This was understandable, because it was illegal for a woman to preach, and they didn't want to be jailed—or worse, burned at the stake. But the way Margery tells it, no matter what happened, the other pilgrims were always wrong—because God was on her side.

In terms of medieval Christianity, Margery Kempe was not extreme. Other religious people cried as much as she did. However, they might not have cried quite as loudly or been quite as aggressive about their piety. Some pilgrims worried that because she cried so much, Margery might be possessed by an evil spirit, while others thought she was drunk or ill. Modern writers have argued just as much as medieval people did about whether Margery Kempe was truly holy, whether she had some kind of disease that caused her to have fits, or whether she was simply a proud and self-aggrandizing woman. We will probably never know the truth. We can say with certainty, however, that she must have been very difficult to live with.

Many of the things that happened to Margery and her maidservant are included in this novel. For example, a number of companions traveled together, one of whom was a priest, and in Cologne, a papal legate took care of Margery, finding her a companion to see her over the Alps. Margery's speech was colorful, and she was given to metaphors that reveal a lot about her life as the daughter of a merchant, such as when she says she would rather be chopped up as small as meat for a pot than not tell religious tales, or when she compares holy things to commonplace ones from her life in Lynn—the sticky skin of boiled stockfish, the sound of a pair of bellows blowing, the song of "a little bird which is called the redbreast." Members of the nobility would probably have used loftier metaphors.

Although the basic outline of the novel follows Margery's memoir, for the sake of the story I have made some changes. The biggest of these is Margery's itinerary.

On this particular pilgrimage, which began in the year 1413, Margery went to the Holy Land before she went to Rome. I took out her visit to the Holy Land. Nevertheless, the overland route that Margery took was one way people got to Rome, partly because of their desire to visit various holy places—such as Assisi, the home of St. Francis—on the way. (This could pay off: praying at some shrines could shorten by years the time you might spend in Purgatory, giving you a faster route to heaven after you died.) There's so much Margery leaves out, including which pass she took to get over the Alps, but she does mention many of the places where she stopped on her route: Norwich and Yarmouth, Zierikzee (in what is now the Netherlands), Cologne, Constance, Venice (where she took a ship to the Holy Land and to which she returned), Assisi, and finally Rome.

What Margery tells us about her maidservant—mostly complaints—allowed me to piece together a great deal of Johanna's story, but who she was, where she came from, and what happened to her after she became the keeper of wine—all of that I had to invent. Johanna sees things from a Christian perspective. Catholicism would have permeated her life. The Reformation, and the beginning of Protestantism, hadn't happened yet, and in Western Europe, almost everybody was Roman Catholic. If you go to the town of Lynn, which is now called King's Lynn, you can see St. Margaret's Church, which Johanna mentions. It's still in use. So is another church, All Saints. You can see the anchorhold attached to it, the small room in which a holy man chose to be walled up to pray for the rest of his life. Walking around King's Lynn, past the medieval guild-hall and through the arched town gate, or listening to the wind blow across the flat salt marshes, you can still hear an echo of what life might have been like in the fifteenth century.

Most of the other characters in the novel are invented. Their names, however, all belonged to real people from fourteenth- and fifteenth-century England, including my favorite, *Iohn mowse, clarke.*

sources

I used many sources while writing this novel. Primary among them was Barry Windeatt's translation, *The Book of Margery Kempe* (New York: Penguin, 1985), from which the quotations in the author's note are taken, and Sanford Brown Meech and Hope Emily Allen's Middle English edition, *The Book of Margery Kempe* (London: Oxford University Press, 1940). Three books about Margery that I found helpful were Clarissa Atkinson's *Mystic and Pilgrim: The Book and the World of Margery Kempe* (Ithaca: Cornell University Press, 1983), Margaret Gallyon's *Margery Kempe of Lynn and Medieval England* (Norwich: Canterbury Press, 1995), and Anthony Goodman's *Margery Kempe and Her World* (London: Pearson/Longman, 2002). Among other very useful books were Barbara Hanawalt's *Growing Up in Medieval London: The Experience of Childhood in History* (New York: Oxford University Press, 1993), Norbert Ohler's *The Medieval Traveller* (trans. Caroline Hillier; Rochester, N.Y.: Boydell, 1989), and Jonathan Sumption's *Pilgrimage: An Image of Mediaeval Religion* (London: Faber and Faber, 1975). John Mouse and Thomas say some things that I took from Helen Waddell's *The Wandering Scholars* (New York: Doubleday, 1955), and valuable information about medieval households came from *The Household Book of Dame Alice de Bryene 1412–1413,* edited by V. B. Redstone (Ipswich: W. E. Harrison, 1931) and Elaine Power's translation of *The Goodman of Paris* (New York: George Routledge and Sons, 1928). A Web site designed by Sarah Stanbury and Virginia Raguin, "Mapping Margery Kempe," includes photographs of the town of King's Lynn and some of its buildings, as well as other information about Margery's life and times: www.holycross.edu/departments/visarts/projects/kempe

acknowledgments

When I think of all the people who contributed in some way to this book, I am humbled. To name each of them would take pages, so here I will thank only a few: Nancy and Bill Barnhouse, Sid Brown, and Allison Wallace for their support and encouragement; Megan Isaac and Lisa Carl for their helpful comments; Robbie Mayes for urging me to keep trying; Diane Landolf for saying yes; and Ena Jones, for being the best critique partner I could ever have imagined. My gratitude to you all.